'There's no problem that I can see, Jassie, my love. You only have to look up to see that.' Ben placed a curled finger lightly beneath her chin and tilted her head upwards.

A sprig of mistletoe hovered over them, the pale, translucent berries a stark contrast to the dark green leaves. 'You see?' he said, his voice a coaxing rumble against her cheek. 'Mistletoe is for lovers…and I'd love more than anything to fulfil its promise… to kiss you and make you mine, just for one delicious moment.'

Ben didn't wait for her to answer, and if the truth were known she couldn't have spoken at all right then. The mistletoe gleamed faintly above them, and she knew that what *she* wanted more than anything was for him to kiss her…a long, sweet and thorough kiss… And, as if he had read her mind, that was exactly what he did.

When **Joanna Neil** discovered Mills & Boon®, her lifelong addiction to reading crystallised into an exciting new career writing Medical™ Romance. Her characters are probably the outcome of her varied lifestyle, which includes working as a clerk, typist, nurse and infant teacher. She enjoys dressmaking and cooking at her Leicestershire home. Her family includes a husband, son and daughter, an exuberant yellow Labrador and two slightly crazed cockatiels. She currently works with a team of tutors at her local education centre to provide creative writing workshops for people interested in exploring their own writing ambitions.

Recent titles by the same author:

THE SECRET DOCTOR
HAWAIIAN SUNSET, DREAM PROPOSAL
NEW SURGEON AT ASHVALE A&E
POSH DOC, SOCIETY WEDDING

PLAYBOY UNDER THE MISTLETOE

BY
JOANNA NEIL

existence outside
ve no relation
e name or names.
any individual
all the incidents

First published in Great Britain 2010
Large Print edition 2011
Harlequin Mills & Boon Limited,
Eton House, 18-24 Paradise Road,
Richmond, Surrey TW9 1SR

© Joanna Neil 2010

ISBN: 978 0 263 21730 8

Harlequin Mills & Boon policy is to use papers that are natural, renewable and recyclable products and made from wood grown in sustainable forests. The logging and manufacturing process conform to the legal environmental regulations of the country of origin.

Printed and bound in Great Britain
by CPI Antony Rowe, Chippenham, Wiltshire

PLAYBOY UNDER THE MISTLETOE

CHAPTER ONE

WHY on earth had she agreed to do this? Jasmine risked a glance down from the lofty platform of the metal fire tower and immediately regretted it. Just looking out from that height made her feel dizzy, and it didn't help that the eager crowd watching from below were way too far away for their faces to be seen clearly. At this rate, with nausea and vertigo both coming into play, she'd very soon be a patient for real, instead of simply acting the part.

'You'll be fine,' Mike had said, in cheerful mood after he had persuaded her to take part. 'You're used to walking the fells in the Lake District, aren't you? And I recall you said you had attempted to climb Scafell Pike and Helvellyn, so this should be no problem at all. We're demonstrating a crag rescue here, and you know how that goes. Forget that this looks like a scaffolding structure. Just imagine that you're stranded on Scafell Pike, and everything will drop into place.'

Jasmine winced at his choice of words. Right now, the notion of anything dropping anywhere was enough to make her stomach plunge all over again. Not that Mike had any qualms about this venture. He was a co-ordinator for the various mountain rescue teams in this part of the country, and of course he would have very few concerns about the exercise.

'It's not at all the same,' she had protested. 'I had time to prepare for those and they didn't present me with a sheer, vertical face…not the bits I attempted, anyway.' She had shuddered. 'I can't think why I let you talk me into it.'

Mike had chuckled. Determinedly optimistic, he had urged her towards the base of the tower and coaxed her up the ladder to begin the ascent, following close behind her.

Which was why she was stuck here now, alone on the topmost platform, pretending to be someone who was lying injured on a crag. Lying injured… The words struck a chord of memory, and she recalled what Mike had said. 'Flail your arms around a bit and cry out for help. The crowd will love that. Then sink to your knees and pretend to topple over. After that, all you have to do is lie still and let the rescue team do the rest.'

So that's what she would do…anything to get this over and done with. She would perform her heart out for the crowd of people who were watching the rescue demonstration from the safety of the fire station's courtyard.

She wrapped her arms around herself in an effort to keep warm. It was not the best of times to be carrying out this operation—a freezing cold December day, with a smattering of snow in the air and the wind buffeting her from all angles.

It was also the final day of her course, marking the end of her week-long stay at the luxurious nearby hotel, and maybe if she lay down and thought about the comforting lounge waiting back there, with its log-burning fire, and the delicious cocktails or the aromatic pot of hot coffee that the waitress would bring, it would take away some of the stress of her present situation.

With that in mind, she went into her act with a bit more enthusiasm. 'Help,' she shouted, waving her arms and pretending to stumble. 'Help me, someone, please, help me. My leg's broken.'

Then she sank to the floor of the platform and waited for her rescuer to arrive.

It wasn't long before she heard sounds of activity coming from the ground below, along with the clink of chains and pulleys, and then, finally, she felt the thud of movement as someone began climbing the tower.

The whole edifice seemed to judder as her rescuer approached, but perhaps it was her overwrought imagination playing tricks on her. The tower was solidly based, wasn't it? It would not topple.

Even so, a faint film of perspiration broke out on her brow. The nausea began to return in full force and she muttered a few curses that should have had Mike squirming in his boots if he'd been anywhere near.

'Whatever did Mike do to deserve all that vitriol?' a deep, male voice enquired, the tone threaded with a hint of amusement. 'Letting loose a plague on him is kind of overkill, don't you think?'

'You wouldn't say so if you were in my shoes,' she retorted, sucking in a sharp breath. 'I could have been watching all this from a safe distance if it weren't for him. I could even have slipped away out of the cold and gone back to the hotel to enjoy a glass of something laced with a warming dash of brandy.'

'You can still do that.' The man swung his legs over the metal rail and dropped down onto the platform beside her. He hauled a metal basket stretcher over the bar, and placed it down on the platform floor. Then he looked at her, taking in her pale features, and in an instant the smile on his face became transfixed, very much as though he had suddenly found himself locked in a time warp.

'Jasmine?' The word was a soft breath of sound. 'Is it really you?' His gaze was fastened on her, his eyes widening as though he couldn't believe what he was seeing.

She stared back at him. 'Ben?' All at once she couldn't breathe. What was he doing here? What did he have to do with the rescue services, and how was it that she should run into him again after all this time?

'How long has it been?' he asked, echoing her thoughts. 'Five years?'

'Something like that.' She frowned. Her jaw was locked in a spasm of disbelief and shock was beginning to set in. She had never imagined that she would ever see him again, but here he was, in the flesh, and even after all the years that had gone by, it was clear that he still had the ability to make her heart pound and cause the air in her lungs to be constricted.

He hadn't changed at all. He was as ruggedly handsome as ever, his black hair neatly cropped to outline his sculpted features, those blue eyes ever watchful and his mouth beautifully expressive, just as she remembered.

'You're down here to take part in one of the courses being run at the Royal Pennant Hotel, I take it? I've been speaking to a few of the people who were attending the medical seminars.' He had come out of his reverie and had snapped back into action in an instant, beginning to prepare the metal cradle to receive its patient.

It wasn't so easy for Jasmine to get back into the swing of things, but she made an effort. 'That's right. "Critical Care and The Role of the First Responder".' This last day was taken up with the activities of the emergency services, and although it wasn't an essential part of her course, she had stayed on to get a better idea of what was involved. It was already on the cards that one of these days her job with A and E might involve her going out on call. In fact, up until now the idea of doing that had been quite appealing.

'We'd better slide you onto this stretcher and

get you strapped in,' Ben said, becoming businesslike. 'People will be wondering what's going on.'

How had he managed to return to his customary efficiency within a matter of minutes? She felt oddly disgruntled. It hadn't taken him long to get over his astonishment at seeing her again, had it? But, then, why should she expect him to be affected in any way by meeting up with her? He had made his final break with the village five years ago, leaving without so much as a backward glance, and why should it matter to him that he had left her nursing a bruised and battered heart?

He frowned, glancing at her briefly. 'Are you all right?'

'Yes, I'm fine.' She wasn't going to let him in on any of her thoughts. Far better that he should remain in blissful ignorance. Ben Radcliffe had the power to unsettle her without even trying, and she had discovered long ago that her only defence against him was to keep her feelings locked away inside her.

She shivered a little as soft flakes of snow began to drift around her, settling here and there on her jacket. 'Shouldn't there be someone else up here with you, doing this work?' she asked.

He shook his head. 'The powers that be planned this as a one-man rescue…for places where there is restricted access. So I'm on my own. But, no matter… I'll splint the broken leg and lift you into the cradle as gently as I can.' He gave a half-smile. 'It shouldn't be too difficult. If I remember correctly, you were always a slip of a girl. It doesn't look as if things have changed very much.'

She frowned. How could he tell? She was wearing a waterproof jacket over a warm woollen sweater and snug-fitting denim jeans. For extra warmth she had added an Angora scarf. She wished she could pull it up over her face so that she could hide away from him, very much like an infant who imagined that with her eyes covered she could not be seen. She didn't want him reading her thoughts and dragging her vulnerabilities out into the open after all this time.

'Are you still living at the cottage?' he asked, deftly strapping splints into place. For extra security, he bound both of her legs together.

'Yes, I am. I never left Woodsley Bridge. I suppose I was fortunate in that I was able to do most of my medical training at the local hospital.' That had been the perfect option for her, but it hadn't done for Ben, had it? He'd started his medical tuition at a prestigious teaching hospital in Carlisle, some eighty miles away from Woodsley, coming home whenever he'd had a few days off just to make sure that his grandmother was all right. Even after she'd died, he'd come back to Mill House once in a while to keep an eye on things, but in the end, when other opportunities had beckoned, he couldn't wait to leave the village behind once and for all.

He glanced at her briefly. 'You always did love being home and having your family close by, didn't you?' His mouth made a bleak downward turn, but it was there only for an instant, so fleeting that she might have imagined it. His good humour was restored almost at once. 'Let's get you onto the stretcher, shall we?'

'All right.'

He knelt down beside her and leaned closer. 'I'm going to put my arms around you and lift you onto it. You don't need to do anything except keep very still. Let me do all the work, okay? We have to do this for real, just in case anyone down there has a long-range camera lens zoomed in on us.'

She made a face. That possibility was more than likely. The press were out in force, along with a team from the regional TV studios, keen to film the day's activities. It wasn't just the people on the course who were interested in what was going on—visitors from all around had come to see the events being staged by the rescue services. The hotel was doing a roaring trade.

He slid his arms around her, cradling her for a moment as he tested her weight, and that was almost her undoing. How many times had she wondered how it would feel to have him hold her this way, only to shy away from that thought? But now it was happening for real, so that she felt the strength of those arms closing around her and became aware of his innate gentleness, and above all she absorbed the warmth of his body next to hers.

'Ready?' His cheek brushed hers as he moved to get a better grip, sending a ripple of flame to run through her veins. In the next moment she was being lifted and very carefully placed on the stretcher. 'Okay, now we need to swing your legs into position. Easy now… Let me take the weight… Remember you have a nasty fracture. As soon as we have you settled, I'll fasten the harness.'

She was glad when the manoeuvre was finished. Every time his hands touched her, to position her or adjust a strap, her body went into meltdown. She wasn't at all sure how much more of this she could handle before she ended up giving herself away. It wouldn't do to have him know how her fickle, treacherous body responded to having him near.

He was the man who'd had the girls back home burning up in a fever of excitement. He'd only had to look in their direction and they had queued up, vying for his attention, and she had vowed she wouldn't be one of them. Ben was never going to stay around long enough to have a long-lasting relationship with anyone, was he? He couldn't even manage to make a go of things with his father.

'Are you all set?' He gave her a fleeting glance. 'I'm going to climb back over the tower and give the signal to the men on the ground so that they can begin hauling on the ropes to lower you down.'

She nodded warily. 'Are you quite sure they're going to hold?' The stretcher rocked from side to side as he tugged on the ropes and raised it up a fraction. Perhaps if she just closed her eyes and imagined she was swinging in a hammock in her mother's garden, this whole nightmare would end.

Her unease must have shown in her expression, because he chuckled softly. 'I'll be with you all the way to steady the stretcher as you make the descent. My harness is attached to the line so that I'll be alongside you. My feet will be on the base rail of the stretcher. Don't worry about a thing. I'll take care of you. Trust me.'

She closed her eyes fleetingly. She had long ago given up on any idea that he would be there to take care of her, or that he would be by her side whenever she needed him. Those were dreams from fantasy-land, weren't they? As her brother's friend, he had always been around, coming to the house, teasing her playfully until warm colour had filled her cheeks...but that was where it had ended. She had always been stranded on the fringes of his circle, looking on from afar, watching him struggle with his own demons and being unable to do anything to help.

He gave the signal to the waiting rescue team and then supported the basket stretcher as it was lifted over the rail. Then he followed, true to his word, accompanying her every bit of the way, his feet resting on the base of the stretcher, his long body leaning over her, his hands guiding the rope that lowered them to the ground. It was strangely comforting having him watch over her that way.

It was all over in a matter of minutes. 'You're safe now,' Ben said, giving her a reassuring look as they reached ground level. 'Home and dry. No worries.'

The people assembled in the courtyard were clearly impressed with the smoothness of the operation, and there were smiles all around. Ben supervised Jasmine's transfer into the waiting ambulance, and then Mike appeared with steaming mugs of coffee. Once she was out of range of the onlookers, the patient miraculously recovered.

Freed from the restraints of the harness, she sat up and looked around at the interior of the ambulance. The windows were darkened and with the doors closed they were spared from prying eyes.

'That was a great show,' Mike said, looking from one to the other. 'A very smooth rescue mission…so you'll be able to go home now and relax.' He paused. 'Until next time.' He grinned at Jasmine's pained expression.

'I don't think you should be having any ideas on that score,' she told him, giving him a look from under her lashes and clasping her coffee mug with both hands so that the warmth seeped into her. 'I'm not likely to be volunteering again any time soon.'

Mike feigned disappointment. 'Are you quite sure about that? I had you pencilled in for at least ten more meetings.'

She frowned. There was no way.

Sitting across from her on the opposite stretcher bed, Ben gave a wry smile. 'Jassie copes well enough on mountain slopes where she can fend for herself,' he said, 'but this is not quite the same. She's never been one to rely on others, so putting herself in someone else's hands must have been quite an ordeal. She's always been an independent soul.'

Jasmine sipped her coffee. His comment startled her. He seemed very sure of himself, as though he knew these things for a fact, so could it be that in the past he had actually been aware of her presence when she had thought him oblivious? It was true they had belonged to a group that regularly climbed the fells, but she had always teamed up with a friend on those occasions, whilst he had been accompanied by his fellow medical students. She frowned. Had he really taken note of what she was doing back then?

'Well, she did a great job today...you both did,' Mike said. He stood up. 'I'll say goodbye, then. Drink up and get warm. I should go and see what the rest of the team are up to...so thanks for your help this afternoon, both of you. I'll look forward to meeting up with you again.'

They nodded and murmured their goodbyes, and Mike left the ambulance, closing the door behind him to keep out the cold wind.

'What will you be doing now?' Ben asked, looking at Jasmine. 'I'm guessing this is your last day, isn't it? Are you planning on going straight back to the hotel?'

She nodded. 'I need to pack up my things and start heading back to the Lake District. It's been a good week, but I'm looking forward to going home. I'm supposed to be helping my mother put up Christmas decorations this weekend, and once that's done I'll make a start on my own place.'

'Are you sure that it's wise to travel that distance in this weather? It's over sixty miles away, isn't it?' Ben was frowning. 'The snow doesn't seem to be clearing up, and if it thickens and starts to settle, the roads could soon be covered. Wouldn't you do better to stay overnight at the hotel?'

'And risk being stranded here?' She shook her head. 'The main roads should stay fairly clear, I imagine, if the gritters have been at work. My room is booked for the night, but I think I'd prefer to set off as soon as possible and take my chances.'

'Hmm.' He studied her thoughtfully. 'So you

won't be staying to have dinner at the hotel before you leave? It had occurred to me that perhaps we might have a meal together and talk over old times.'

She hesitated a moment before answering. From the way he was talking, he must believe that everything that had gone before was simply water under the bridge. The fact that his thought-less actions had ruined her brother's life hadn't made so much as a dent in his confidence, had it? Or perhaps he felt that enough time had passed, the situation had changed, and they could all go on as if nothing had happened. For her own part, she couldn't make up her mind whether he was entirely to blame for what had gone on. She was fiercely loyal to her brother, but sometimes life didn't turn out quite the way people wanted.

'That would have been something to look for-ward to,' she answered softly, 'but I daren't risk any delay. I just have to stop by the hotel to pick up a suitcase and some packages—I managed to do quite a bit of Christmas shopping while I've been staying here. It seemed like too good an opportunity to miss, looking around the shops in a different town.'

Still, the thought of sitting down to eat a hot meal before she set off was very tempting right now—she wasn't even going to think about how it would be to stay with Ben for a little while longer.

As an afterthought, she added, 'But perhaps I could ask room service to send up a light meal and we could talk while I do my packing? After all, it probably wouldn't be wise to start the journey on an empty stomach, would it?'

As soon as the words slipped out, she was regretting them. What had possessed her to suggest such a thing? Was she mad? He was her brother's sworn enemy, a heartbreaker with no conscience, and here she was, actively encouraging him to spend time with her...and in her hotel room, at that. Had she taken leave of her senses?

'I'd like that,' Ben said, a look of satisfaction settling on his features. 'I'll follow you back there, just as soon as you're ready to leave.'

'I'm ready now.' She'd already burnt her boats, so she may as well go where the tide led her. 'As you say, the weather's not good, so it would be as well not to delay too long.' She stood up, taking time to adjust her scarf before picking up her empty cup and heading towards the door of the vehicle. Ben responded swiftly, unfurling his long body from the seat and going after her.

They went to the car park, and from there they started the journey to the Royal Pennant Hotel. Ben followed her for some two miles along the Yorkshire roads until at last they turned into the hotel's wide forecourt. He drove carefully, she noticed, all the time mindful of the road conditions. The snow had turned to sleet, making the lanes slippery and treacherous.

She wasn't looking forward to the long drive home. Her small car was reliable, but it wasn't built for good manoeuvrability in snow and ice. His car, on the other hand, was an executive-style, midnight-blue saloon, built for power and road-holding capability.

It was a relief to arrive at the hotel, and the

grand entrance hall was more than welcoming. It positively enveloped Jasmine with its warmth, reflected in the glow of polished mahogany timber, the sweep of luxurious carpet, and the orange and gold flames of the fire that crackled in the huge fireplace.

'My room's up on the first floor,' she told Ben. 'I'm lucky in that I have a small sitting room set apart from the sleeping area, so we'll be able to eat in comfort.'

'That sounds ideal.'

Once they were in the room, Jasmine waved him to a seat by the table, and then took off her scarf and jacket and laid them over the back of a chair to dry.

'This is a lovely room,' he commented, looking around. 'It's all very tastefully decorated.'

She nodded. The curtains and upholstery gave it an elegant but homely feel, and everything was pleasing on the eye.

Ben glanced beyond the sitting room to where part of the large double bed was visible, its counterpane matching the fabric of the curtains.

'It's good that they've separated the sleeping area from the living area with a narrow wall partition—it tends to give a notion that they are individual rooms and yet keeps the general feeling of spaciousness.'

'Yes, it does. I was really pleased when I first saw the room. I wouldn't have chosen to be away from home, but I've been comfortable here, and I have everything I might need, like a phone, desk and writing materials. I also brought my laptop with me so I've been able to sit here of an evening and type up my notes from the course.'

She ran a hand through her long, burnished chestnut hair, tossing her head slightly, allowing the waves to ripple freely. It was good to be uncluttered by her outer garments, and for the first time that day she took a deep, satisfying breath, content to be back in the cosy confines of her room.

'Perhaps you'd like to order room service for both of us,' she suggested, 'while I start on my packing?' She glanced at Ben as she went to place her suitcase on the bed, but something in his gaze made her stop what she was doing.

He was watching her closely, a glimmer of pure, male interest in his blue glance as it trailed over her, taking in the silky sweep of her hair and wandering down to trace a path over the gentle curve of her hips.

'I'd almost forgotten how beautiful you are,' he murmured, his gaze returning to settle on the soft curve of her mouth. 'Whenever I thought about you, I'd remember your smile, the way you had of looking at me with that guarded expression, as though you weren't quite sure what trouble I'd land myself in next. But it was always your hair that fascinated me. It's so glorious that I'd long to run my fingers through it, very much as you did just then.' He smiled. 'Only I would have lingered a while longer, I think.'

His gently seductive manner unsettled her, causing her to falter as she set the suitcase down on the bed. Had he really been thinking about her from time to time? She hadn't expected that. How was she to deal with this man from her past now that he had turned up, out of the blue, the one man she had kept at a distance all this time for fear of being hurt? He'd been a charmer, a man who'd known exactly how to wind women around his little finger, and it didn't seem as though much had changed.

She fumbled with the zip of the suitcase, encountering resistance, and within a second or two Ben was beside her, his hand resting briefly on hers. The fleeting contact caused a tide of heat to surge through her veins and brought a soft flush of colour to her cheeks.

'There you are,' he said. 'It's free now.'

'Thank you.' She tried breathing slowly and deeply for a while in an effort to calm herself down. She studied him, letting her gaze run over his features and trying to assess what really lay behind that calm, unruffled exterior. 'It's been a while since we last ran into one another,' she murmured, struggling to find her voice. 'I'm surprised that you thought about me at all.'

'It would be hard not to think about you,' he responded with a faint smile. 'After all, we both lived in the same village, and I watched you grow from a lively tomboy who landed in almost as many scrapes as I did into a lovely, serene and accomplished woman. It would have been very strange if I had forgotten you after that, just because we were separated by a few miles.'

She gave him a long, thoughtful look. Was he teasing her, trying to lead her along the same route that all those unsuspecting young women had travelled back home…like Anna, her brother's girlfriend? She had to be wary of him. He simply wasn't to be trusted.

'Like I said, maybe you should order some food for us…the menu is on the desk. I'll have a jacket potato with cheese, please. And a pot of coffee would be good. I've a feeling I'll need something to sustain me on the journey.'

He nodded, accepting her change of subject without comment. Glancing through the menu, he said, 'I think I'll go with the ham and cheese melt. Leave it with me.'

She nodded and turned back to her packing. Some fifteen minutes later, she had managed to cram most of her belongings into her case, and Ben lent a hand with zipping it up.

'All this for one week?' he murmured, lifting a questioning brow. 'How can any woman need so many changes of clothes in such a short space of time—unless, of course, you've been throwing yourself wholeheartedly into the night life? A few boisterous nights in the bar with the people on your course?' He was looking at her quizzically, and she shook her head, giving off an air of innocence. He lifted a dark brow.

'Well, maybe a couple,' she amended with a laugh. 'Though they weren't what you'd call boisterous...more of a lively and animated type of evening, I'd say, especially as the night wore on.'

His eyes took on a contemplative expression. 'No intimate dinners for two, then? Does that mean you're not involved in any serious relationship at the moment? Or maybe you've a boyfriend waiting for you back home?'

She frowned. Why did he want to know that? There was no way she was going to let him wheedle his way into her affections, was there, given his past history? Enough was enough, and she decided to sidestep his questions. Why should he learn every detail of her private life when she knew nothing of his? Simply guessing what he might have been up to was bad enough.

'It means,' she said, looking down at her overstuffed case, 'that I've packed my suitcase full of the Christmas presents I've bought for friends and family while I've been up here. Like I said, I couldn't resist the opportunity to explore the shops in a new town…and with Christmas just three weeks away, there was no time to lose, was there?'

His mouth curved. 'I guess not,' he said, accepting her avoidance tactics with good enough grace. Then he moved away from her as a waiter arrived with the food, setting it out on the table.

'I ordered a couple of desserts, too,' Ben told her when the man had gone. 'All this is my treat,' he said. 'I told the receptionist I would be paying for it.'

'Thank you…but you didn't need to do that.' She eyed up the mouth-watering fruit crumble topped with creamy custard and felt all her good intentions fade away. How had he known that was her favourite? 'That's my diet blown for the week,' she added mournfully.

He laughed. 'I don't believe that you've ever needed to diet in your life,' he said, looking her over. 'You've a perfect hourglass figure…'

She steeled herself not to rise to his bait. 'Perhaps you should sit down and eat before the food gets cold,' she suggested, doing her best to bat his comments to one side. 'And tell me how it is that you came to be working with the rescue services this afternoon. I thought you were working in A and E, the same as me.'

She pulled out a chair and sat down opposite him at the table. Glancing out of the window she could see that in the grey light of the afternoon the snow was beginning to thicken, fat white flakes coming down in a steady flow.

'I wanted to try something different,' he said, taking a bite out of his toasted sandwich. 'I used to enjoy climbing in the Lake District and thought I might volunteer my services for the mountain rescue team. Then one of the team members here fell sick, so Mike asked me to come and do today's stint. I suppose that's why you didn't see my name on the advertising bumph.'

She nodded. 'I wondered if it was something like that.' She scooped up a mound of potato. 'I expect you know most of your local team already, don't you? That will probably make things easier for you, won't it?'

He shook his head. 'I won't be working with my local team because I'm preparing to go back to Woodsley. I've served out my notice at the hospital where I've been these last few years.'

Jasmine put down her fork and stared at him. 'You're going home? After all this time?'

'That's right. I might not be too welcome back there, but five years has perhaps been long enough for me to stay away. There are things I need to deal with, and I think it's probably high time I started to put my life in order.'

She pressed her lips together. The news had come as a huge shock. How was she going to cope if Ben came back to the village? Woodsley Bridge was a relatively small place, and the chances of seeing him around and about were pretty great. There would be no escape.

Even so, she couldn't prevent the thrill of nervous excitement that shimmied along her spine at the thought of him coming home. But that was the unruly, wanton side of her body betraying her, wasn't it? Common sense told her that there would be nothing but trouble if Ben went back to the Lake District. How would his father react?

Worse still, how would her brother Callum deal with the wanderer's return? Once, he and Ben had been best friends, but all that had changed. He blamed Ben for taking Anna away from him, and that anger had not dissipated. It had continued to simmer throughout all those long years.

How was she going to deal with this? Was she destined to stand on the sidelines and watch the process of bitter condemnation start all over again?

CHAPTER TWO

JASMINE frowned, gripping the steering-wheel firmly and making a determined effort to concentrate on her driving. Starting out on the long journey home, she was still reeling from the bombshell that Ben had dropped just a short time ago.

Her mind was caught up in a fog of confusion. One minute she had been secure in her own sheltered world, and now, in an instant, everything had changed. Somehow, she couldn't come to terms with the fact that from now on he would be staying around. For her, life in her home village of Woodsley Bridge would never be quite the same again.

It was early evening now, already dark, and snow was falling in a gentle curtain, lending a picture-postcard atmosphere to the landscape.

The branches of the trees were topped with thick ribbons of snow, the rooftops of isolated farmhouses had become a pristine white and all around snow spread like a glistening carpet over the fields. It was lovely to look at, but not so good when she had to drive in it.

She had already been on the road for half an hour, and there were still many miles left to go. She was keeping her fingers crossed that the steady downfall would ease off at some point and that at least the roads would stay clear.

Ben was following her on this first lap of the journey. 'My route follows yours for the first fifteen miles or so,' he had told her before they'd set off, and she had looked at him in surprise.

'But I thought you were living in St Helens, down in Cheshire,' she responded with a frown. Surely that was in the opposite direction?

Driving along, she recalled their conversation. 'I didn't realise you knew where I was living,' he had said, raising a brow.

She'd given a faint shrug. 'Information filters through from time to time about what you've been doing or where you are. People might have caught a glimpse of you, here and there, or maybe their friends and relatives have been further afield to a hospital for treatment…it really doesn't take much for word to get around.'

He'd smiled crookedly. 'Tongues will always wag, won't they? I expect rumours are rife about all my transgressions. The village folk could never quite get over my youthful misdemeanours, could they? *That Radcliffe boy's up to his tricks again* is about all I ever heard from them. Even when I was doing my medical training they were convinced I'd be thrown out for something or other.'

He wasn't far off the mark there, Jasmine acknowledged inwardly. His father had made it clear from the first that he wasn't expecting him to finish the course, and perhaps that was because his son had such a wide range of interests that he found it hard to stick to one in particular. Ben was a wild spirit, always game for anything, and even at medical school he had managed to raise brows. News of his exploits quickly found its way back home.

'Well, you did get into trouble for almost setting fire to the kitchen in your student residence,' she murmured. 'And then there was that time when you and your friends stayed out all night and turned up at your lecture next morning looking the worse for wear.'

He made a face. '*Almost* being the operative word about the fire,' he said. 'I only left the omelette cooking on the hob for a minute or two while I went to help a fellow student who had cut her hand…and the fact that the smoke alarm didn't go off was down to someone else removing the battery and forgetting to put it back. I think he was fed up with it going off every time he made toast.'

His brows drew together. 'And as to the night out, why should that have turned out to be a disciplinary offence? At least we turned up for the lecture on time next day. Some of these people on the boards of universities seem to have no recollection of what it's like to be a student. Yet

I'll bet they had their moments, if the truth was known.'

'You make it sound as though it was all unfair,' she said with a wry smile. 'Anyway, I'm sure that's all in the past. I heard you'd done well for yourself in the last few years. There was a piece in the paper about you setting up a new emergency paediatric unit at the hospital in Cheshire…' She frowned. 'But that brings me back to what I was saying—if you're following the same route home as me, I'm guessing you must be living and working somewhere else at the moment.'

He nodded. 'I've been doing some locum work up in Lancashire, so it made sense to stay there for the last couple of months. And, of course, it meant I was able to come and do the stint with the rescue services today, since I'm based not too far away.'

It made sense to Jasmine. He had always been a restless soul, and from what he had just described of his travel arrangements, things didn't seem to have changed very much.

Now, though, she glanced in the rear-view mirror and saw that he was still following behind her, his beautiful car eating up the miles without the slightest hint of difficulty. She wasn't so lucky. Her own car had been throwing up problems along the way.

The outside temperature had dropped to below freezing, and it seemed that her tyres were not up to the job of gripping the slippery surface. She had to take extra care on the bends in the road, and as if that wasn't enough, the snow was still coming down thick and fast so that her windscreen wipers were struggling to clear it away.

The roads were becoming increasingly clogged with snow as drifts began to pile up along the hedgerows, and now she was worried that she might not be able to go on much further. Perhaps Ben had been right when he'd suggested she should stay overnight at the hotel.

Still, she wasn't the only one who had decided to venture out. A few drivers were following the same route, doggedly determined to get home.

She looked at the road ahead. The car in front of her was negotiating a bend, and as the road sloped downwards the driver seemed to have trouble maintaining a straight course. He swerved as the car in front of him suddenly drifted in an arc across the road, the unexpected action causing him to veer wildly. A second or two later, he rammed his vehicle sideways into a large oak tree. Still in a skid, the other car swivelled around, hitting his front end and coming to a halt halfway across the road.

Jasmine's stomach clenched and her pulse began to quicken. Her mouth went dry and she was uneasily aware of the thud of her heartbeat as it rose up into her throat. How was she going to avoid being part of the pile-up ahead? Both cars were taking up a good half of the road directly in front of her, and she wouldn't be able to stop in time to avoid them. She couldn't brake or she would go into a skid, too. She had no choice but to go on.

Her mind was racing. She was all too conscious of Ben not far behind her, and she didn't

want to risk him being caught up in any colli-
sion. Her only hope was that, with any luck, he
would have seen what was going on, and would
be able to find some way of avoiding trouble.

She wasn't going fast, but now she changed
to a lower gear, slowing the car and carefully
steering through the only gap available between
the cars and the hedgerow. Thankfully, no one
was coming in the opposite direction. Then, as
she tried to steer a course away from trouble, the
camber of the road changed, throwing the car
out of kilter in the bad conditions, and a moment
later her vehicle slewed violently around, slam-
ming her headlong into a snowdrift.

The car shuddered to a halt, tipping over at an
angle, and she stared at the windscreen, seeing
nothing in front of her but a blanket of white.
Apprehension clutched at her insides. It seemed
very much as though she had plunged part
way into a ditch, and maybe the hedgerow had
stopped her going any further. Her heart plum-
meted. Now it looked as though she was going

to be stranded here, miles away from anywhere, in a dark, frozen void.

The engine had cut off. There was silence all around, and it seemed as though she was enclosed in a capsule, shut away from the outside world. It was eerie and scary at the same time, being trapped in this pale wasteland.

'Are you okay?' A moment or two later, Ben was pulling at the door of her car while she was still trying to take stock of everything that had happened.

Relief washed over her. Ben was safe and she wasn't alone. 'Yes,' she answered, struggling to keep her voice level. 'I'm okay.'

'You're quite sure that you're not hurt in any way?'

'I'm sure. I'm not hurt.' She blinked, looking around at the overwhelming mass of snow that covered three sides of her vehicle like a half-built tunnel. She tried to gather her thoughts. 'Did you manage to keep your car on the road?'

'It's fine. I've parked just along the road from you.' He hesitated. 'If you're positive that you're all right, I need to go and check on the other drivers. If we don't clear the road fast, there could be another accident before too long. We have two people keeping watch, so that they can try to alert people to the danger, but it isn't safe and I need to hurry.'

She nodded. 'I'll come with you.'

'There's no need.' As she tried to slide out of her seat, he laid his hands on her shoulders, lightly pressuring her to stay. 'You look as though you're in shock,' he said. 'You're trembling. Stay there and I'll be back as soon as I can.'

He was right, she realised after he had gone. Her body was still mourning the loss of his reassuring touch, but that was only because she was in a state of shock, as he'd said…wasn't it? She tried to move, but her legs let her down and her hands were shaking. Her car was slanted at an odd angle to the ground and she wasn't at all certain how she was going to get it back on the road.

For a minute or two, she sat very still, concentrating on breathing deeply in an effort to compose herself. No matter what he said, Ben most likely needed help. If they didn't move the other car to the side of the road, it would be a danger to oncoming drivers. It was also quite possible that one or both of the people involved in the accident might be injured. Sitting here wasn't an option, and somehow or other she had to pull herself together and try to help out. Bracing herself, she drew another shuddery breath of air into her lungs, and a moment later she slid out of her seat and went to find him.

He and another man were trying to steer the crumpled car to the side of the road, but the vehicle that had rammed into the tree was still in the same position as before. The driver was at the wheel, and she guessed that Ben must have already spoken to him. The man wasn't moving, but perhaps that was because he was traumatised by what had happened.

She went over to car and opened up the passenger door. 'Is there anything I can do to help you?' she asked. The man was in his fifties, she guessed, with a weathered complexion and streaks of grey in his hair. His expression was tense, as though he was hurt and was steeling himself against the pain. 'I can see that you're holding your arm,' she murmured. 'Is it giving you some problems?'

He nodded, his lips compressed. 'I wrenched it when I went into the tree. Help's on its way, though. The man from the BMW told me he's a doctor...he came to take a look at me and said I'd probably dislocated my shoulder. He had to go and shift the car out of the way, but he's coming back.'

'I'm sure he'll be able to help you.' She quickly tried to assess his condition. He was wearing a cotton shirt with a sleeveless fleece jacket over the top, and even in the darkness she could see that the shoulder was strangely distorted. 'He and I know one another, as it happens—we're both doctors.'

He managed a weak smile. 'I suppose I'm lucky, then, that this happened while you were around.'

'You could say that.' She hesitated. 'Is it all right if I switch on the interior light? Perhaps I could take a look at you and see what we're dealing with?'

He gave a slight nod, and once the light was on she examined his arm and his hand. 'Can you feel your fingers?'

'I don't think so. They're a funny colour, aren't they?' He frowned. 'That's not good, is it?'

'Well, it means we probably need to put the shoulder back in its socket sooner rather than later. Your circulation is being stopped or slowed down, and we have to sort it out fairly quickly.'

She glanced around and saw that there was a cushion on the rear seat. 'If we put the cushion between your arm and your chest it may help to make you feel more comfortable in the meantime.'

He nodded again, and she went to get the cushion, coming back to gently place it in position. A faint look of relief crossed his features.

'That feels a bit better,' he said, breathing hard and gritting his teeth. 'Thanks.'

'You're welcome.' She glanced at him. 'Are you hurting anywhere else? I noticed the driver's door is buckled…has that hurt you in any way?'

'I don't think it's done anything too bad. It feels as though I'll be bruised for a while, but basically I'm okay. It's just the shoulder. It hurts like the devil.'

'I can imagine it does.' She hesitated momentarily. 'Will you be all right for a minute or two while I go and get my medical bag from the car? We should be able to put your shoulder back in position for you—and we can at least give you something to relieve the pain.'

'That would be good.' He seized at the chance. 'Whatever you can do…'

'Okay.' She slid out of the car once more and trudged through the snow to her own vehicle, thankful that she was wearing strong leather boots.

'What are you doing?' Ben asked, coming

over to her, his brows drawing together in a dark line as she retrieved her bag from the car. 'I thought I told you to stay where you were. At least you would have been warmer in there, and you know you shouldn't be wandering around when you've just been involved in an accident. You could be injured and not realise it.'

'I'm a doctor,' she said in a succinct tone, her green eyes homing in on him. 'I think I'd know if there was something wrong with me.'

'Not necessarily.' His gaze lanced into her. 'You should let me check you over.'

She raised both brows. 'We both know that's not going to happen.' Just the thought of him laying hands on her was enough to make colour sweep along her cheekbones. She just hoped he couldn't see her reaction, and to avert disaster she went on, 'It looks as though only one man was injured. Apparently, you said you'd go and help him.'

'That's right.' He studied her briefly, and clearly he must have decided not to pursue the point about her staying in the car.

'Well, it looks as though his circulation's compromised, so I think it would be best to try to put the shoulder back in place here and now, rather than wait.'

'Yes, that's pretty much the conclusion I came to.'

Jasmine was thinking out a plan of action. 'In that case, he'll need a sedative and a painkilling injection,' she added. 'I have the medication we need in my medical bag.'

'Good. You're right, it will probably be best to inject the joint, rather than set up an intravenous line and anaesthetise him. That way, he would be knocked out completely, but his recovery would take longer, and these aren't exactly the best of circumstances for him to be undergoing that kind of treatment.' His gaze ran over her once more. 'We could do it together, if you think you're up to it…?'

'I am. I'll be fine. I'll support him while you do the reduction.'

'Okay, then. Let's go and see how he's doing.'

The injured man, they discovered, was

becoming paler by the minute, and his lips were beginning to take on a pinched appearance.

'Ian,' Ben said, slipping into the passenger seat beside him, 'we're going to give you something that will help you to stay calm and relaxed throughout the procedure, and then I'll inject a painkiller directly into the joint. The drugs will help to relax your muscles at the same time. All that means you shouldn't feel too much discomfort when I put the bone back into place. You should feel immediate relief from pain when that's done.'

Ian's lips moved in what they took for agreement. 'Anything,' he said. 'Please, just put it back so that I can start to think straight again.'

They worked together to give him the medication and prepare him for the manipulation. Then they manoeuvred him from the driver's seat to where they could work more comfortably. Jasmine positioned herself to one side, getting ready to stop any sudden, untoward movement as Ben popped the shoulder back into its socket.

As soon as it was over, Ian slumped back in his

seat. 'Thanks,' he said. 'That was really painful until you two set to work.'

Jasmine was pleased to see that his fingers had started to regain their normal colour, which meant his circulation had been successfully restored. 'You need to keep the shoulder very still,' she told him. 'Any movement will cause more damage.'

Ben had been searching through his own medical bag and now he brought out a shoulder sling. 'This should help to immobilise the joint while it heals,' he said. 'The tissues around the shoulder will probably be inflamed and swollen for a few weeks, so I'll prescribe some anti-inflammatory tablets for you. I can give you some to be going on with, but you should get the shoulder checked out at a hospital as soon as possible. They'll probably do an X-ray to make sure that everything's okay…and they'll want to make sure that you have no other injuries.'

Ian nodded. 'Thanks. Though I don't know how I'm going to get to a hospital in this weather. I don't even know how I'm going to drive…or even if the car is capable of getting me anywhere.'

'Same here,' Jasmine said. 'Mine's halfway down a ditch. It seems we're both in the same boat.'

'Wretched weather.' Ian grimaced. 'I suppose I could call for a taxi…we could share, if you like. That's if anyone will come out in this weather, of course.'

'There's no need for that,' Ben put in. 'I can help out. My car's not damaged in any way, so I can drive both of you. Actually, there's a cottage hospital with a minor injuries unit not too far away from here. They have X-ray facilities, so they should be able to sort you out.' He looked at Ian. 'I'll drop you off there, if you like, and maybe you could call a relative to come and pick you up later?'

Ian thought things through. 'I expect my son will come once he finishes work. He's on the late shift, but he has a four-wheel drive, so I don't suppose he'll have too many problems with the road conditions.'

'What about you, Jasmine?' Ben's gaze rested on her. 'You're not going to be able to make it to Woodsley Bridge tonight, are you? I can put you up at my place overnight, if you want. At least you'll be warm and safe there, and we can make arrangements to have your car towed to a garage in the morning.'

A surge of relief flowed through her. 'Thanks,' she said, giving him a quick smile. 'I'd appreciate that, if you're sure you don't mind? It's getting late, and it's a weight off my mind, knowing that I won't have to start making all sorts of arrangements at this time of night.'

'Good. That's settled, then.' Once he had everyone's agreement, Ben was ready for action. 'We'll load your luggage into the boot of my car and get under way.'

He helped Ian into the BMW, making sure that he was secure and comfortable in the back seat. 'The hospital's a couple of miles down the road,' he said. 'We'll have you there in just a few minutes.'

Jasmine sat in the front passenger seat,

absorbing the sheer luxury of Ben's car. Everything about it spelled comfort and opulence. The temperature was perfect, the seats were heated, and the upholstery gave off a rich scent of supple, new leather. There was even soft music playing in the background.

It all lulled her into a false sense of security, making her feel as though everything was right in her world and that it was perfectly normal for her to be sitting here next to Ben. She tried not to notice how his strong fingers closed around the wheel, or the fact that his long legs were just an inch or so away from her own. The material of his trousers pulled across his powerful thighs, drawing her attention, and she quickly looked away.

When they arrived at the hospital, they went with Ian into the casualty department and waited while a triage nurse took details of the accident and organised an immediate appointment for him in the X-ray department. Then Ian rang his son, and once they were confident that arrangements were in place for him to be picked up later that evening, they said goodbye to him and set off for Ben's house.

'It isn't too far away,' Ben said, as he turned the car into a country lane. 'We've had to make a bit of a detour, but we should be there soon. I'll rustle us up something to eat—it seems like an age since we had that snack back at the hotel.'

She gave a crooked smile. 'I know what you're thinking… I should have stayed there and agreed to have dinner with you. It would have saved all this trouble.'

He sent her a sideways glance. 'I wasn't going to say that…far be it from me to say I told you so.' He grinned. 'But sitting down to a relaxing dinner with you and taking time to catch up with all your news would have been good.'

She sighed. 'I know. But I did so want to get home.' He didn't need to know how wary she was of being in close proximity with him for any length of time. 'It's just that my mother will be putting up the Christmas tree tomorrow evening, and it's sort of a tradition that I help her with the baubles and decorations. I love this time of year. We always have Christmas carols playing in the background while we dress the tree, and my dad brings us hot liqueur coffees and warm mince pies, so that we really get into the festive spirit.'

She smiled. 'Of course, he complains that he's not really ready to celebrate three weeks early while he's still working, but as a GP he could be tending patients on Christmas morning, so we tend to ignore that and get on with it.'

Ben grinned. 'Your father has always been a solid, easygoing man, though, hasn't he? Nothing ever really fazes him. I suppose that comes from taking care of all the folk in the village for years on end and dealing with their quirks and foibles.'

'That's true.' She sent him an oblique glance. 'What about you? Will you be going back to the manor house to stay with your father?'

He shook his head and his expression became sombre. 'I don't think so. That wouldn't go down too well. My father and I have never seen eye to eye over anything very much.'

'But you'll be spending Christmas with him, won't you?' She frowned. 'Now that you're going home, surely he'll be glad of the chance to see you again after all this time? Perhaps you'll be able to forget what went on in the past and try to start over again.'

'It sounds good in theory,' Ben said. His mouth flattened. 'But, truthfully, I don't suppose he'll welcome me with open arms. He can be stubborn at the best of times.'

'I'm sorry. That's so sad.' Her green eyes clouded. 'It's such a shame to see a family torn apart at the seams when maybe a word or two could put matters right.'

His expression was cynical. 'Do you really imagine that I haven't tried?' He shook his head. 'I know you mean well, Jassie, but you should give up on trying to reconcile my father and me. I've come to the conclusion that it isn't going to work. I've written to him, tried to talk to him on the phone, but he's brusque and uncooperative, and I have the feeling that I'm wasting my time. It's not even as if I'm the one in the wrong…

well, not totally, anyway… But it doesn't seem to make any difference to how he thinks and feels.'

His mouth made a flat line. 'Things were said, on both sides, that should have been left unsaid, and the damage has been done. The wounds they leave behind never truly heal.'

'I don't believe in giving up,' she murmured. 'Not where family is concerned, anyway. I'd always be looking for an opportunity to put things right.'

His expression softened. 'That's because you're a sweet, generous-natured woman who only ever looks for the good in people. I'm just afraid that before too long you'll find yourself disillusioned, and that would be a terrible shame.'

She absorbed that, subsiding back into her seat without comment. The only way she had ever been disillusioned had been in her dealings with Ben. Over the years, she'd watched him, wincing as he'd made his mistakes, biting her tongue when she'd wanted to speak out about his various entanglements, wondering if there would ever be a time when he would look at her with the light of love in his eyes.

But that had been asking for the impossible—how would he ever have done that when she'd constantly shielded herself from him for her own protection? Besides, she had long ago given up on that dream world. Life had thrown a spanner in the works when Ben had gone away with Anna.

She could never keep up with Ben. He had been like quicksilver, constantly on the move, rising to challenges as and when they'd arisen. All his youthful energies had been fuelled by rebellion against the hand life had dealt him… losing his mother at a very young age had been a raw deal, the worst, and who could blame him for his confusion and disenchantment with life? No wonder he'd run amok through the village in his tender years and stirred up a storm.

Knowing all that, maybe it was the reason why Jasmine had always looked beyond the vigorous, determined exterior to what lay beneath.

Her feelings for him had never changed. They just became more impossible to manage as time went on.

CHAPTER THREE

'THIS is it,' Ben announced after a while, turning the car into a snow-filled drive. 'My house—I usually think of it as my summer place, since I mostly use it for holiday breaks or those times when I need to get away from it all…but the title doesn't exactly fit at the moment. Still, I hope you'll like it.' He cut the engine and turned to face Jasmine. 'Let's get you inside and into the warm.'

'Your summer place—does that mean you're not renting short term, that this is actually your own house?' She was puzzled. 'After all, you must have a house in Cheshire as well, if that's where you've been living for the last few years.'

'That's right. I bought this as a run-down

property some time ago and spent a year or so doing it up.'

'So renovating properties is one of those interests that you kept up? Working on Mill House back in Woodsley Bridge was just a start?'

'That's true. I've always been enthusiastic about restoring houses...ones that particularly interest me, that is.'

She frowned. 'I wasn't sure whether your father would have put you off. He didn't go along with any of it, did he?'

He made a wry face. 'Unfortunately, my father and I don't see eye to eye on a number of matters. With Mill House he was convinced I was wasting my time...and money...and he did everything he could to put me off starting the work. Even though it was a successful restoration in the end, he maintained it was money that could have been spent on more solid investments.'

She nodded. 'He couldn't understand why you went to all that effort, could he?'

'No. But, then, sentiment never came into his calculations.'

Jasmine understood Ben's difficulty. Stuart Radcliffe never had time for such creative projects. He was an old-fashioned man, putting his faith in good bookkeeping and heavily involved with upper-crust institutions. Ben's ideas were very different, stemming from the heart, and Stuart could not go along with that. To him they were risky, pointless ventures, whereas he was all about safety and security.

Ben held open the door for her and she slid out of the car, looking around at the broad sweep of the drive and the sprawling white-painted house. It was set in open countryside, and as the moon cast its light over the snow-laden fields, she caught a glimpse of hills and dales and gently forested slopes all around.

She looked closely at the house. She could see why Ben would want to work on this lovely old property. Clearly, it had stood the test of time, and now, with a fresh coat of paint and what she guessed were renovated windows and roofing, this was a splendid example of what could be achieved.

'Of course, you're not seeing it at its best in this weather,' he commented as he went to retrieve her case from the boot. 'If you were to come here in the summer you would see it in its full glory.'

'I think it's lovely.' She dragged her gaze back from the scenery to the front of the house. A lantern glowed in the wide porch, welcoming them with its golden light, and to either side there were hanging baskets, filled to the brim with winter flowers. There were pansies, big, bright blooms of deep violet, azure blue, burgundy and stunning orange. Mixed in with those were purple-leaved sage and long stems of trailing ivy. It was a glorious explosion of colour that said no matter that it was winter, plant life was exuberant and thriving.

He put his key in the lock and opened the front door, ushering her inside and placing her case on the floor by a decorative plant stand. Ferns filled the shelves, their vibrant green a charming contrast to the mellow wood. The hallway was large and inviting, with a deep-piled carpet and walls that were covered with delicately textured paper that was pleasing on the eye. To one side there was a Georgian satinwood table, beautifully inlaid and elegant with delicately curved legs. A bowl of vivid red cyclamen provided a splash of rich colour that was reflected in a large, gilt-framed mirror that hung on the wall.

'I'll show you to the living room,' Ben said. 'I've laid a fire in the hearth, so once I light it the place will be much more welcoming. The central heating's on, so we'll be warm enough.'

'I'm toasty already,' she said. 'The heat enveloped me as soon as I walked through the door.' She was still looking around, trying to take everything in. 'This house must be…what… seventeenth century?' There were exposed oak beams all around, and an oak staircase led to a mezzanine floor that could be seen from the hallway. Even from where she was standing, she could see through the wooden rails of the elevated balustrade that the upper level had been tastefully furnished with comfortable chairs and an antique desk. All around, the lighting was subdued but warm, throwing out soft pools of light here and there.

He nodded. 'It is…late seventeenth.' He showed her into the living room, where the centrepiece was a huge fireplace, made of beautifully polished wood topped with an intricately carved cornice. 'I tried to restore it carefully, keeping the original features intact wherever possible.' He bent to light the log fire and stood back after a minute or two, waiting as the flames took hold. The logs began to crackle and throw up orange and gold sparks, sending a pool of light into the room. 'That should soon make things more cheerful,' he said.

'This is so wonderful,' she told him, looking around in awe. There was a richly upholstered sofa close by the hearth, along with matching armchairs, and it was easy to see that Ben's flawless taste in furnishings was innate and impeccable. There was an elegant bookcase to one side of the room, complemented by a glazed

Georgian display cabinet and a small occasional table.

'It's such a treat to see a place like this,' she said, full of admiration for what he had achieved. 'You must have worked so hard to make it look this good.'

'It took a fair bit of time and effort,' he agreed, smiling. 'Let me take your jacket and then you should make yourself comfortable on the sofa while I start supper. I'll show you around after we've eaten, if you like.'

'I would love that, thanks…but perhaps I could help with the food? There must be some way I can make myself useful.'

He mulled it over. 'Perhaps you'd like to do the salad? The ingredients are mostly ready prepared, so they just need to be tossed together in a bowl with some dressing. Just give me a minute while I take your case upstairs and put the car in the garage.'

'Okay.'

The kitchen, she discovered, was another perfect combination of golden oak units, granite worktops and a quarry-tiled floor. It should perhaps have been cold, given the type of floor covering, but under-floor heating meant that it was warm and inviting.

'I thought we might have a couple of grilled steaks along with pan-fried potatoes,' Ben said, a slight frown indenting his brow. 'Does that sound all right to you? You haven't gone vegetarian on me in the last few years, have you?'

'Not yet,' she murmured. She rolled her eyes. 'Steak sounds like heaven to me. I'm starving.'

'Good. Then we'll get started.' He switched on the grill and fetched steaks from the fridge, and within a very short time they were ready to sit down to a feast. The steaks were cooked to perfection, and he added mushrooms and tomatoes so that the whole meal was mouthwateringly delicious. Jasmine's salad was a crisp mix of lettuce leaves, bright peppers, radish and coleslaw.

'We could eat in the dining room, if you like,

but sometimes the kitchen has a much cosier feel,' Ben said. 'What would you prefer?'

'This is just fine by me,' she murmured, looking around. There was a small square table to one end of the kitchen, with stylish, high-backed oak chairs that lent a touch of distinction to the breakfast area. This quiet, uncluttered area exuded an atmosphere of comfort and relaxation, and she could imagine Ben sitting here of a morning, eating his breakfast and reading the newspaper.

'So, tell me what you've been doing with yourself these last five years,' Ben said, waving her to a seat and setting out the plates of food. 'You've mentioned you were working in A and E, and obviously you're interested in furthering your career, as you were doing the course in critical care.'

'That's right.' She added a helping of salad to her plate. 'I'm working as a senior house officer at Wellbeck Hospital. I've been there for a number of years now, so it's almost like home to me, and I get on well with everyone there.

I've never particularly wanted to work anywhere else.'

'Does the fact that you attended the course mean you're thinking of branching out?' He sliced off a piece of steak and started to eat. 'I mean, were you thinking of going out with the rescue services?'

'Maybe. I've been giving it some thought. Only perhaps I'll go as a volunteer to begin with. I know the local team could do with extra hands, especially people who are medically qualified. They used to have a doctor on call, but he recently retired, so they're looking for someone to take his place.'

'Yes, I heard about that.' He poured wine for both of them. 'Actually, they've already found his replacement.' He looked at her intently, and there was almost an expectant quality about his expression.

She returned the look, frowning, and then her eyes widened. 'Are you telling me that you're going to do the job?'

He nodded. 'It's really only an extension of

what I've already been doing in Cheshire. I'll be on call with the local team, as well as acting as a first responder in cases where the emergency services need a doctor to arrive on the scene fast. The rest of the time I'll be based at Wellbeck.'

'Wellbeck?' Jasmine gasped. She couldn't stop that small explosion of sound. 'You mean we'll be working together?' She laid down her fork and stared at him, trying to take it in. A pulse began to throb heavily in her throat. 'What kind of role will you be taking on there? Is it a permanent post?'

'It's temporary. It's just a short-term contract, for a couple of months, filling in for the specialist registrar in A and E while he's over in the States.'

Slowly, her heart rate began to return to normal. It was such a shock, learning that they were to work together. It was one thing to know that he would be living near her, but to be seeing him every day at the hospital where she was based was altogether a different thing.

She picked up her fork and let it hover over the mushrooms on her plate.

'Don't tell me I've managed to put you off your food?' Ben queried lightly. He was watching her, his gaze moving over her as though he could read and understand every detail of her expression. 'You and I will manage to get along well enough, won't we?'

'Of course. I mean... I... It was so unexpected. I'm not sure what I thought you would be doing back at Woodsley, but for some reason it didn't occur to me that you would be coming to the local hospital. One of the hospitals where you did your training, perhaps, in Carlisle or Edinburgh, but Wellbeck was never top of your list of preferences before, was it?'

'Times change, people change,' he said with a negligent shrug. 'The opportunity arose and I decided to grab it.'

'But why now, after all this time?' She swallowed some of the wine, aiming for Dutch courage and feeling it warm her all the way to her toes. Or perhaps the warmth was merely as a result of the fact that he was sitting opposite her and she had no way of escaping that penetrating stare. He knew how she felt about having him around. He had picked up on her guarded responses, and he knew full well that her alarm systems were on full, chaotic alert.

'I heard that my father was ill.' He said it simply, in a matter-of-fact tone. 'He wouldn't have told me himself, of course, but word filtered back to me via friends in the know.'

'I hadn't heard anything about that.' Jasmine frowned. 'My father's his GP, but of course he wouldn't have said anything to anyone. I've seen your father out and about from time to time, but I didn't realise that he was sick.' She looked at him, her gaze troubled. 'Is it serious?'

'I'm not sure. All I know is that he's seeing a specialist about problems with high blood pressure. It's possible that hypertension could have affected his kidneys, but I don't know anything for certain.' He pressed his lips together. 'I'm not surprised…he was always uptight and on edge, not the best recipe for good health.'

'I'm so sorry. You must be very worried about him. What are you going to do?'

He shrugged. 'I don't know. Somehow I'll have to find a way of keeping an eye on him. Blood is blood, after all, and there's no denying the fact that he's my father. I shan't rest easy unless I know I've done everything in my power to make sure he's all right, whether he wants my help or not.'

She reached for him, laying her hand on his. 'It must be so difficult for you…he's never been an easy man to get along with, and now you're disrupting your life so that you can do the right thing. I hope you can make him see sense and put all the bad feeling behind you for once and for all.'

'So do I.' He gently squeezed her hand, drawing her fingers into his palm. He was warm and vibrant, his inner strength transmitted to her as if a special bond had been created between them. It was as though he had drawn her into his embrace and wrapped her in his powerful masculine presence.

Then he reluctantly broke the link between them, and Jasmine struggled to bring her thoughts back to some kind of order. It suddenly came home to her that she was here, in his house, dining with him, and in all the years she had known him she would never have dreamed of sharing this precious moment of intimacy with him.

She would even be sleeping under the same roof as him, and only now did it occur to her that she needed to keep an especially tight watch on her feelings. It would be all too easy to fall for Ben. Even after all these years, when the folly of a youthful infatuation had passed, there was still a lingering pool of yearning, a soft tugging at her heart that told her she could come away from all this with her emotions in tatters.

He moved away from the table a short time later, clearing away the plates and stacking them in the dishwasher. 'I can offer you fruit salad for dessert, along with cream or ice cream, or perhaps you'd prefer something more substantial, like treacle sponge and custard?' He lifted a brow in query.

'Fruit salad would be lovely, thanks…with ice cream.' Her mouth made a crooked shape. 'It seems the wrong season to be wanting that, but I could eat it all year round.' She sighed. 'I wonder if the snow is easing off at all? I rang the garage to ask if they would pick up my car for me, and they said they would try to do it tomorrow. I've no idea what damage might have been done—but at least the insurance company will offer me a hire car while it's being repaired. I'm just wondering if I'll still be able to make it home tomorrow.'

He lifted the blind at the window and peered outside. 'There are just feathery flakes coming down now. I expect the snowploughs will be hard at work tonight, and if the worst comes to the worst and you don't want to drive, I could take you home. I could do that anyway, if you like. I have to be back here on Monday, because my locum job finishes and I need to hand over to my successor, but I can't see any problem. Either way, we'll make sure that you get home.'

Her mouth curved upwards. 'Thank you for that. I owe you. I'm beginning to be really glad that I met up with you today.'

'Even though it stirred up a few demons?' His blue gaze glittered as he placed the dessert in front of her. 'I would always look out for you, Jassie. You have to know that. You were the only one who never condemned me, whatever I did…apart from my grandmother, of course. She was always on my side…a real treasure, a gem of a woman with a heart of gold. She had lots to say about what I should do and how I should conduct myself, but she never forced her opinions on me or berated me when I made the wrong choices. I think she had faith in me that if I followed my own instincts, things would generally turn out all right.'

He sat down once more and began to eat his own fruit salad. 'And mostly they did, except where my father was concerned.'

'I liked your grandmother.' Jasmine remembered the dear old lady who had lived close by her father's surgery. She had been Ben's maternal grandmother, a cheerful, lively woman who had always been busy making jam or doing craftwork for the village fete. 'We used to talk sometimes, whenever I went by Mill House, or we would meet up in the village sometimes. She was thoughtful and kind...and she always had time for people.'

'She had a lot of time for you.' His face was sad and his eyes clouded with memories. 'She used to call me when I was away at medical school and tell me about the things you'd been up to. I heard all about it when you decided to train as a doctor, when you passed your finals and bought your cottage, even about the various young men you dated from time to time.'

Jasmine blushed. 'She didn't! Why would she even mention that to you?'

'Perhaps because she knew I'd be interested.' His gaze slanted over her, taking in the silky swathe of her hair and the clear green of her eyes. 'You always steered clear of me, and I can't say that I blamed you, but I was definitely keen to know what type of man caught your attention. I can't say I approved of some—I was pretty sure their intentions were none too good—but then my grandmother pointed out that people in glass houses shouldn't throw stones.' He smiled. 'She was a shrewd woman, my gran.'

'She was, but you obviously didn't take her up on any of her advice.' She had recovered herself by now, and was ready to fend off any more comments he might throw her way. He knew she was vulnerable, and he would play on that. Ben was a master of the art of winding women around his little finger. He would find a way of creeping under her guard without her even realising what he was doing.

They finished off the meal in the living room drinking coffee by the open fire, and she asked him about his work in the A and E unit in Cheshire and how he had come to set up the new paediatric unit.

'One of my specialties was working with children,' he said. 'It wasn't very satisfactory, treating them alongside adults who were injured, so we thought of ways we could partition off a separate area for them. We had child-friendly murals painted on the walls and provided play activities for those with minor injuries. The most important thing was that we recruited staff who were trained in paediatrics. In the end, the management was so impressed with what we'd done and with how smoothly it worked that they arranged funding for a permanent children's A and E department.'

'That must have given you a lot of satisfaction,' she acknowledged. 'We're lucky at Wellbeck, because we have good facilities there for both adults and children.' She hesitated, dipping her spoon into the chilled mix of pineapple, grapes and peaches. 'I would never have expected you to choose to work with children.'

She had no real idea how Ben would interact with the little ones in his care. His skills as a doctor weren't in doubt, but looking after sick and injured children was difficult for the best of the medical profession, let alone someone who had no real experience of how youngsters behaved or reasoned. After all, Ben was an only child who'd lost his mother when he had been five years old…and he had no young nephews or nieces to show him the way. And yet, against all the odds, he seemed to have succeeded in what he'd set out to do.

'I find it exhilarating sometimes,' he said. 'Children have no artifice. They say it as it is, and you always know exactly where you are with them. And when they recover from what-ever ails them, they bounce back at full steam, ready to get on with whatever takes their fancy. It can be truly rewarding, working with them.'

'I can imagine. I just never thought I would see you in that role.'

They talked for a while longer, and then he said on a questioning note, 'Would you like to see the rest of the house?'

She nodded. 'Yes, please. Actually, after that I'd be quite happy to settle for a good night's sleep. It seems to have been an unusu-ally long day.'

'It's certainly been eventful.' He smiled. 'I'll show you to your room.' He stood up and started to walk towards the hallway, commenting lightly, 'There aren't a lot of rooms, as you've probably already gathered. Downstairs there is the living room, kitchen, dining room and a bathroom, and of course you've seen the mezzanine floor. That's what I think of as my study—I have my desk and computer up there, and there's a bookcase so that mostly everything I need is to hand.'

'I noticed it as soon as we arrived. It looks so peaceful up there, and all that golden oak adds to the feeling of comfort and well-being.'

'I think so, too. I enjoy knowing that a good deal of the house is made up of natural materials. I tried to keep true to that theme upstairs, with the same exposed beams and oak floors for the hall areas. There are three bedrooms, one with an en suite bathroom, and there's a separate bathroom between the other two.'

He led the way up the stairs, and she was truly impressed by the love and care that had gone into making this house a home. The master suite was decorated in gentle tones of blue and grey, with small items of exquisite antique furniture providing storage or seating.

'I thought you might like the larger of the two guest bedrooms,' he said, showing her into the room. 'It faces out onto the garden, so you have the sun in here a good deal of the time.' He watched her expression as she gazed around. 'Will you be all right in here, do you think? There's mostly everything you might need, and you'll find a washbasin and toilet set into the recess. There wasn't room for a proper bathroom, but you can always use the one next door if you prefer. Either way, I've put out soap, towels, shampoo and so on. Just give me a shout if there's anything I haven't thought of.'

'It's absolutely perfect,' she told him. 'I love the soft cream and gold colours in here. It's a lovely room.' There was even a small escritoire where she could sit and write if she wanted… not that she had any intention of doing that, but it was a delightful addition to the room.

'I'm glad you like it.' He came to stand beside her, sliding an arm around her shoulders. 'Of course, if you should change your mind…if you decide at any time that you'd rather come and share with me, you're more than welcome. There's actually nothing I'd like better.'

His comment took her breath away…quite literally. Not only that, he was standing so close to her, not pressuring her in any way but so near to her that she felt the brush of his thigh against hers, and her soft, feminine curves were gently crushed against his long body. She loved the way he was holding her, but her nervous system was already signalling danger, clamouring a warning, while all the time her foolish body was firing up in feverish response.

Slowly, with infinite care, he drew her closer, his hand coming to rest on the gentle curve of her hip. He lowered his head and sought out her lips, and in the next moment he was kissing her, a tender, sweet exploration that rocked her to the core of her being. His hands stroked along her spine, urging her even nearer to him, and as her breasts softened against his chest and her thighs brushed against his, she knew that she was standing on a virtual precipice.

Her heart was pounding, her whole body overwhelmed by a hot tide of longing. She wanted, more than anything, to take up his gentle invitation, but after years of watching him from afar she knew all too well that this could be her undoing.

'Ben…' She mumbled the words against his lips, and ran her hand shakily over his hard rib cage. 'Ben, I can't do this…' Even now, her traitorous body was trying to cling to him, desperate for one last moment of exquisite fulfilment, and perhaps he recognised that because he kissed her again, trailing his lips over hers and scorching a path along the slender curve of her throat.

'But you want me…' he said, his voice roughened with the edge of desire. 'I feel it with every heartbeat, with the way your body softens against mine. Take a chance, Jassie…just this once, let your heart rule your head. I won't let you down, I promise you. I'll take care of you. I'll make sure that you're all right. I'll keep you safe.'

If only she could believe him. If only she could let go of all the bonds that held her back. Would it be so wrong to spend this night with him, to taste for once the joy of being with him in the one way that really mattered?

But how could she trust his promises? Hadn't he said those same things to Anna years ago? And where was she now?

How would Callum feel if he knew that his own sister had betrayed him with the one man who had destroyed his dreams? She couldn't do it. Her peace of mind would be destroyed for ever and there would be no going back.

She laid her hand, palm flat, on his chest. 'I'm sorry,' she whispered. 'It just wouldn't be right. You and I could never be together.'

For a moment or two, he stayed very still. Then he seemed to pull himself up, as though willing himself to move away from her. He rested his cheek against hers, his breathing ragged as he registered what she was saying.

Then he reluctantly eased himself away from her. 'It's okay,' he said, his gaze meshing with her troubled green eyes. 'Don't worry about it. I should have known better.' His mouth made a crooked downturn. 'It's just that I've waited such a long time to see you again, Jassie, and you're exactly as I remembered…such a beautiful woman, so gorgeous I couldn't believe you were actually here with me. I couldn't help myself.'

He held her at arm's length. 'But I'll behave myself from now on, I promise…or at least, I'll try my very best,' he amended hastily, a slight frown knotting his brow. 'Perhaps you'll have to forgive me one or two minor lapses. I'm not—'

'I think perhaps you should stop right there,' she murmured, sending him a shrewd glance. 'You're digging yourself into a hole.'

He gave a husky laugh. 'I am, aren't I?' He studied her fleetingly as though trying to imprint her features on his mind for one last time. 'Try to get a good night's sleep, Jassie.' He frowned. 'For myself, I doubt I'll manage it. I think I'll probably be taking a long, cold shower.'

CHAPTER FOUR

'BREAKFAST should be ready in about twenty minutes,' Ben called, knocking on the bathroom door just as Jasmine stepped out of the shower. 'Is that okay with you?'

'That's fine, thanks,' she answered, wrapping herself in a towelling robe. Her long hair fell in damp waves below her shoulders, and she wondered belatedly how she was going to get it dry as there was no hairdrier in her room.

'Do you have everything you need?' Ben asked, and she was just about to mention the hairdrier when he added on a thoughtful note, 'Could you do with someone to wash your back, perhaps...or maybe you could use some fresh towels? I'm sure I could find some and bring them to you. It's no trouble at all...I'm only too happy to help out in any way I can.' His voice was huskily coaxing, deep and intensely masculine, stirring up all kinds of wild imaginings in her and sending fiery signals darting along her nerve endings. She was all too conscious that there was only a thin door separating them.

'I can see that your good intentions didn't last long,' she said, a hint of amusement in her tone. 'Obviously the cold shower didn't work.'

'That's because I kept imagining you in there with me, and before too long, the water turned to steam,' he said mournfully, but his words took on a tinge of hopeful expectation as he added, 'Are you absolutely sure you don't need any help in there?'

'I'm quite sure, thanks.'

'That's a shame…' He gave an exaggerated sigh. 'Still, nothing ventured, as they say.'

She wrapped her hair in a towel and smiled to herself at his persistence. 'But I could use a hairdrier if you have one,' she told him. 'Otherwise I'll let my hair dry naturally.'

'Hmm.' He seemed to be giving it some thought. 'There's definitely one up here somewhere. Have a look in the second guest room. That's most likely where it is. I'd find it for you, but the bacon's cooking downstairs, and I'd better not risk a repeat of the omelette fiasco.'

'Of course you shouldn't. That would never do, would it? You've spent too long working on this house to have it go up in flames.'

'Too right,' he said. A moment or two later, as she heard him padding down the stairs, she began to quickly dress, pulling on fresh jeans and a cotton top that clung to her curves.

Then she tidied up the bathroom and went into the guest bedroom to look for the hairdrier.

She'd seen the room briefly when Ben had shown her around yesterday evening, but now she took a moment to look at it more carefully. This room was only a little smaller than the one she was using, but it was partitioned into a main bedroom and what appeared to be a smaller dressing room. It wasn't being used as such, from the looks of things when she went to investigate, because there was a small, single bed in there, almost like a child's bed.

The décor throughout both rooms was exquisite, with pale gold fabrics offset with sparing touches of dark red and the palest of greens. The carpet was the colour of sand, and the furniture was the same oak that had been used everywhere else in the house.

There was a dresser by the window, and Jasmine went there first of all to look for the hairdrier. She didn't see it among the collection of fragrance bottles and hand lotions on the tabletop, but it was always possible that it might be in one of the drawers.

She opened the uppermost drawer and straight away found what she was looking for. Smiling, she lifted the hairdrier out, and then glanced at the various bits and pieces that lay beside it. There was a hairbrush and comb, some ornamental hair clips and a small jewellery box containing a couple of bead necklaces and a set of earrings.

She closed the lid of the box, a small frown

starting up on her brow. Next to the box there were a couple of picture books, the sort that might be read by a young child with his mother.

It was all very odd. Were these mementos of Ben's own mother, and relics from his child-hood? Somehow, she didn't think so. The books were reasonably modern, and the jewellery was the sort that you could probably buy on the high street these days.

A more likely explanation was that Ben had a girlfriend who stayed here from time to time... Anna, perhaps? After all, his relationship with Callum's girlfriend must have been serious enough for him to risk alienating Jasmine's brother and at the same time cause more bad feeling between him and his father.

It was common knowledge that Stuart Radcliffe had not been pleased when his son had decided to go off and...in all likelihood... set up house with a young woman from the vil-lage. He didn't go along with a lot of the ways of the twenty-first century. He was a man of high moral standards and his son's behaviour went against the grain.

But Anna wasn't living with Ben now, was she...unless she was back at his house in Cheshire?

It was all too much for Jasmine. She was getting a headache just thinking about it, and she closed the drawer and went back to her own room to finish getting ready.

'You made it,' Ben said as she went into the kitchen a few minutes later. He looked her over, his blue eyes lighting with approval. 'You look fantastic. A man's dream come true, all lissom and lovely—and I can see that you found the hairdrier. It looks as though your hair's made of pure silk. It's beautiful.'

'You never lost the art of charming your way around women, did you, Ben?' She gave him a wry, speculative glance. Did he imagine she would fall for his easygoing, seductive manner? Anything was possible, of course, but she had just had a nasty reminder about why she should steer clear of getting too deeply involved with him. He was a man who was constantly on the move, flitting between people and places with reckless abandon.

His expression became thoughtful. 'You don't seem to be in too good a mood, all of a sudden. Are you worrying about your car, or about getting home, maybe?'

She shook her head. 'No. I'm sure that will all be sorted eventually.'

'That's right. I thought it might be best if I take you home, as the snow's still lying about. I expect you'll be able to pick up your car in a day or two, won't you?'

She nodded. 'Yes, my father will probably bring me back here to collect it.'

She glanced around, seeing that he had laid the table for breakfast and that the food was ready to be set out on the plates that were warming under the grill. 'I feel guilty that you've done all this… I meant to get up early and help with everything, but that mattress was so soft I curled up like a baby and just didn't want to wake up. I'm annoyed with myself.'

He laughed. 'If you slept overlong, then you probably needed it. Come and sit down at the table and I'll serve up. We've bacon, eggs, tomatoes…and there were some fresh mushrooms left from yesterday, so I've cooked them, too.'

'It sounds wonderful…smells wonderful, too.' She sat down and saw that he had made toast and set out marmalade and apricot preserve. There was also a pot of coffee, giving off a satisfying aroma that mingled with the appetising smell of cooked bacon.

'Shall I pour coffee for you?' she asked. She could do with a reviving cup. It might help to sweeten her sour mood. He had been right when he had picked up on her unhappy frame of mind, but she didn't even understand herself why she was out of sorts. Why should the ins and outs of his private life bother her? He had never hidden anything from her. Relatively speaking, his life was an open book.

'Thanks.' He put a plate down in front of her and then went to take a seat opposite her. He started to eat, and then asked softly, 'So if it isn't the travel arrangements that are bothering you, what else is giving you grief?'

She passed the coffee across the table to him. 'Nothing at all. If anything, I'm just reflecting on things, that's all.' Her gaze met his. 'I found the hairdrier in a drawer with all sorts of bits and pieces—some jewellery, a hairbrush… Of course, it's perfectly natural that you should have people to stay with you, or even live with you, but I couldn't help wondering if those things belonged to Anna.'

He nodded. 'Yes, you guessed right. She stays here from time to time and uses the place for holidays, short breaks and so on.'

So he did still keep in contact with her. Jasmine slowly absorbed that piece of information, a small frown indenting her brow. 'And the books?'

He seemed puzzled. 'Books?'

'Children's picture books. They were in the drawer alongside the other bits and pieces. Does Anna have a child? Is that why there's a single bed in the dressing room?'

'Ah, yes. They would be Kyle's storybooks. I didn't realise that she had left them behind.' Ben paused awkwardly for a moment. 'He's four years old, a great little boy but a whirlwind of activity. It's hard to keep up with him sometimes.' He swallowed some of his coffee and then replaced his cup on its saucer. 'I have a photo of him. Would you like to see it?'

She nodded slowly. All at once her appetite had disappeared and the food began to taste like cardboard in her mouth.

His jacket was draped over the back of a chair, and now he went to forage in the pocket, drawing out a leather wallet. 'There he is,' he told her, handing her a small photograph showing an impish young boy laughing into the camera. He had the same black hair and blue eyes as Ben, and as she carefully studied his picture, Jasmine felt as though a little piece of her had died.

'He looks like a lively youngster…a happy-go-lucky kind of boy,' she murmured huskily. She studied the photograph a moment longer before handing it back to him. 'Is he your son?'

He appeared to be taken aback by her question, hesitating a moment before asking, 'What makes you say that?'

'Isn't it obvious? He looks a lot like you. You and Anna were an item…still are from the sounds of things. So it doesn't take much to draw conclusions from that, does it?'

'No, apparently not. Though I wouldn't say that Anna and I are still involved in the way you imagine. I look out for her and obviously for Kyle, too. She doesn't have any parents or any family to turn to, and so I feel it's up to me to make sure that they're both all right. I do what I can for them.'

She noticed that he hadn't answered her question, but for the moment she left that to one side. Perhaps, for some reason, he was reluctant to acknowledge his role in Anna's life, and given the recriminations that had followed the pair, she couldn't really blame him for that. 'You always looked out for her. Isn't that why you gave her the job at the Mill House Bakery once it was restored?'

He shrugged. 'She seemed the ideal person to take charge there. She was young, certainly, but she loved baking and was very good at producing wholesome food. She was also good with people and had a way of charming the customers.'

He picked a slice of toast from the rack and began to butter it. 'My gran thought she would be the perfect person to run the place. Of course, Anna always looked in on Gran at Mill House and made sure that she was all right, so they got on really well. She had a homely way about her, Gran said, and she knew how to pretty up the tea shop and make it welcoming.' He smiled. 'Besides, Gran had a yen for Anna's oatcakes. She said they were delicious served with cheese or pâté.'

'That was true. I tasted them myself. And as to your grandmother's advice, she was a wise lady and above all she was a good judge of character.' She started to eat once again, pricking the egg with her fork so that the yolk spilled out. 'So what is Anna doing now? After all, she left all that behind her when she went to Cheshire with you.' He had put someone else in place to keep the business going, a middle-aged woman with a flair for patisserie, and the enterprise was still thriving.

'Anna runs her own catering business from home, supplying specialty cakes, biscuits, gingerbread men, and so on. It works well for her, because it means that she can keep an eye on Kyle while she's baking. He's just started school, though, so I suppose she'll have more time to herself from now on.' He frowned, spearing mushrooms with his fork. 'That's perhaps a good thing, because she's been finding it difficult to cope lately. She's not well…in fact, she hasn't been well for a long time.'

Jasmine felt a rush of concern. Whatever she thought about the triangle of Ben, Anna and her brother, she had always liked the girl that Callum had brought home. He had said that she was the one for him, and she and her parents had welcomed her to the fold.

'What's wrong with her? Is it something that she's talked about? I noticed that she often tired easily, and maybe she was a little breath-less sometimes, but she never complained and I thought perhaps it was just that she'd been overdoing things, working late in the bakery. She was always looking for ways to improve the layout of the tea shop or add new products to the menu.'

He hesitated before answering. 'She has a con-genital heart problem…though she won't thank me for telling you that, and I hope you'll keep it to yourself.'

She gave a soft gasp. Then she nodded. 'I will, of course.' She frowned. 'Is she having treat-ment for it?'

'Some medication to regulate the heartbeat. The condition was diagnosed some years back, and I think the feeling was to wait and hope that it wouldn't be too problematic. Unfortunately that turned out to be a false hope. She's been seeing her original consultant back at Wellbeck on a regular basis, and he's of the opinion that she's going to need surgery fairly soon.'

'I'm so sorry. I had no idea.' The news was

troubling, and she was sad, imagining what Anna must have had to contend with over the years, more so now that she had a young child to bring up. It was very likely that being pregnant and giving birth would have put an added strain on her heart. 'I can't think why she didn't want anyone to know what she was going through.'

His lips made a flat line. 'Anna is a very private person. There was a good deal of bad feeling when she left Woodsley Bridge, and she was concerned that she had hurt Callum deeply. Personally, I think that concern was misplaced. He had it in his power to win her back, but instead he chose to let her go.'

Jasmine pulled a face. 'I'm not sure that he could have competed with you. Everyone knew you only had to click your fingers and the girls would come running.'

His mouth twisted. 'You're exaggerating. Like most people in the village, you're looking at the surface picture and not delving into what really goes on.'

'Am I? Maybe.' She gave a dismissive shrug.

'Is Anna's need for privacy the same reason why you won't admit to being Kyle's father? Does Anna want you to keep it to yourself? I don't understand why either of you would need to do that.'

He swallowed more coffee. 'That's just the way it is,' he said, his face becoming serious. 'I'll abide by Anna's wishes. What matters is that I knew that I could take care of her, and I promised her that I wouldn't let her down.'

'But you didn't marry her?' Perhaps that was why he didn't want to acknowledge the child was his. Surely any decent man would want to provide for his child, and it would be shameful for him to admit that he had been unwilling to make a proper commitment to Anna?

His gaze met hers. 'No, I didn't. Anna wanted her independence, and I can understand that. She lost her parents at an early age and was brought up in foster-care. Perhaps that's why we get along so well together. It seemed that we had something in common, with me losing my mother and my father being so distant…

and I could understand how she felt when she was striving to rise above her background. She wanted to find her own way in life, but she was vulnerable and she needed a helping hand to get there. I was happy enough to provide that helping hand.'

Hadn't he sidestepped the question once more? Jasmine frowned. Perhaps she was right in her summing-up. He wouldn't own up to being the father because he hadn't been prepared to make a proper commitment to the child's mother. How would that information go down in a small village like Woodsley Bridge…and, furthermore, how would his father react? It would be one more blow to any chance of recovering that relationship.

Whatever the ins and outs of the situation, it was clear that Ben still cared very deeply for Anna. He was still concerned about her five years after they'd left Woodsley together, and he kept a picture of the little boy in his wallet. How much more did she need to know?

'I'm sure she must be thankful for all that

you've done for her,' she said, straightening up, 'just as I appreciate all that you've done for me. Are you sure it won't put you out, taking me home?'

He shook his head. 'Not at all. I want to take a look at Mill House and make sure everything's ready for me to move in. I've been leasing it out for the last few years, but the tenants moved out a month ago. I thought I would air the place and make sure the fridge and freezer are stocked up.' He held up the coffee jug and offered to refill her cup.

She nodded. 'Thanks.' She studied him. 'Are you not going to suggest to your father that you stay with him, at least for a while?'

'And risk a third world war? I don't think so.' He spread marmalade onto his toast. 'Besides, I have my own place, Mill House, and it will be easier to supervise the work on my next renovation from there.'

'Your next renovation? Does that mean you've bought another property?' She raised a brow. 'Do I know the place?'

'The old barn next to the mill. I've been doing a two-storey conversion. There's a stable block there, too, and I'm planning to turn it into some kind of business unit. There's a lot of land with the prospect of development.'

She frowned. 'I heard something about that. There was talk around the village when the for-sale sign was taken down and I know a lot of work has been going on there. I think a lot of people are worried about what kind of business will be started up.'

'And when they find out that I'm the one who has bought the land and property, they'll have even more to say on that score, I expect.' His mouth slanted. 'It doesn't bother me. I'll listen to what they have to say and I'll try to address their concerns, but at the end of the day I have planning permission and that gives me the right to do what I want.'

'Don't you always do that anyway?' She put down her knife and fork. 'What kind of business are you planning? Another shop unit, like the bakery and tea shop?'

'I'm not sure yet. There are certain limitations, given the natural surroundings, but I'm thinking something agricultural. A farm shop, maybe. There's a lot of land attached to the barn and outbuildings.'

'That'll be interesting...in more ways than one.' She gave him a thoughtful glance, and he chuckled.

'You want to see me get my comeuppance, don't you? I can see the headlines now in the village paper: *Woodsley ne'er do well comes unstuck with his latest project. Villagers in outcry over plans to turn place of natural beauty into business hot spot. Traffic jams predicted as outsiders pour in from all around the county.*'

'You may well scoff, but perhaps you need to rethink your approach...more softly-softly might work better than bull at a gate. People are more likely to respond to quiet reasoning.'

'Try telling that to my father.'

She sipped her coffee, watching his expression change to one of sad resignation. 'I know he objected to you restoring Mill House and bringing back the water mill into working order, but you went ahead anyway, so you could hardly say that you lost out.'

'That wasn't what the argument was about.' His lips compressed, as though he was dredging up a painful memory. 'He didn't care that it had been my grandmother's home for years. To him, it was a waste of time and energy to do any work on it. To me, it was the chance for my gran to stay in the house where she had lived with my grandfather for most of her married life. It was the opportunity for her to live in comfort for the remainder of her years.' He frowned. 'I would do it again, without a second thought, if I was presented with the same choice.'

She gave him a gentle smile. 'If it's any consolation, I think you did the right thing. Your grandmother was so happy to be able to stay in the house. I know it must have been hard for you, because it was common knowledge your father put obstacles in your way. I'm not sure exactly what he did, but I know it meant you delayed going to medical school, and you carried out the renovations in spite of him.'

He stood up and started to clear away the breakfast dishes. 'He didn't want me to go to medical school. He said I would never see it through, that it would be one of those fly-by-night ideas that would disappear in a matter of months.'

His mouth twisted. 'Of course, he was set on me going into finance like him, and when I chose not to go to university to study economics and accounting, he held back the money from my trust fund. He had the power to release some of it when I was eighteen, and again when I was twenty-one, but he refused to do it. It was a kind of blackmail, but I called his bluff. And once he'd stated his position, he couldn't back down. Or wouldn't.'

'So how did you find the money to do the work on Mill House?' She put down her coffee cup and began to help him stack the crockery in the dishwasher.

'I took a job with a computer company in town.

There was training on the job, and soon I was earning quite a good salary. I saved as much as I could and put it to use doing the renovations. I did most of the work myself, with help and advice from experts, so in the end it didn't cost too much. And then I had the idea of starting up the bakery next door and selling the products in the teashop. It all worked out pretty well.'

'And that funded your medical studies?'

'That's right. It meant that I started a few years later than I would have liked, much the same as Callum did with his studies, but I managed it in the end, so it all ended well.'

'Except that you never made things up with your father.'

He shrugged. 'I suppose it was a matter of pride with him. I'd gone against him, and he had difficulty coming to terms with that. Even though I qualified as a doctor, it wasn't the profession he would have chosen for me. And I couldn't forgive him for his attitude towards my gran. He liked Gran well enough, but he had tunnel vision and he couldn't see why she wanted to stay in that house. It wasn't a profitable option, he said. It was pure folly to cling on to it, he thought, and he said it was silly sentiment. He had no time for that.'

He closed the door of the dishwasher and began to set the controls.

It was a battle of wills that went on and on between them, Jasmine conceded as she started to straighten the chairs. The final straw, she recalled, had come when Ben had gone away with Anna. Perhaps Stuart had mourned the fact that his son was finally leaving the village. The fact that he was taking Anna with him was one last hurdle he hadn't been able to overcome.

It was also the stumbling block that had tripped Jasmine. How could she even think of trying to get closer to Ben when Anna was still part of his life?

CHAPTER FIVE

'How does it feel to be coming back to Woodsley Bridge?' Jasmine sent Ben a sideways glance as he drove along the country lane leading towards the village. 'I always love to see it as we approach along this road. From the top of the hill the whole place is laid out before you…all those hills and dales and lovely white-painted houses mixed in with stone built cottages… And then there's the sea, shimmering in the distance.'

'It's a pretty place, I'll give you that, even more so when the sun's shining, as it is now.'

She nodded agreement. 'The snow's just about gone from the rooftops, and the sky's such a lovely blue. It's exhilarating. I love it here. The view never fails to take my breath away.' She turned to him. 'But you didn't tell me how you feel about it. Are you having mixed feelings about coming back to the Lake District after all this time?'

He hesitated for a moment. 'I think I am. On the one hand it's good to see the place, but on the other I'm not so sure I'll be welcomed with open arms in some quarters…my father, your brother, the villagers who object to me buying up the land next to the mill.'

She understood how he felt. 'It was never going to be easy, but at least you've taken the first step. Will you be dropping in on your father?'

'Yes. I have to. In fact, I'll probably make that my first call—get it over and done with and see how the land lies after that. I rang him to say that I would be stopping by.'

'How did he react to that?'

He grimaced. 'It's hard to tell. He's not exactly welcoming me with open arms—I'm certainly not the prodigal son redeeming myself in his eyes.' He shot her a quick glance. 'He was fairly noncommittal, I suppose…though I did tell him I'd heard he was ill and wanted to check that he was all right.'

'That must have pleased him, surely—the fact that you cared enough to come back and find out?'

'Probably not. He said he was okay and he didn't need people fussing over him. Then again, he was always a man who preferred to keep himself to himself. I doubt he's going to change very much at this late stage.' He turned the car into the village and headed down a winding road. 'I'm not certain where you want me to take you…would you like me to drop you off at your place, or would you prefer to go straight to your parents' house?'

His smile was crooked. 'I'm assuming you don't want to come back with me to Mill House, of course. If you did, it would be great if we could spend some more time together.'

She smiled. 'Now, there's a dilemma. I'd love to hang around with you for a bit longer, and I'd like to see the house again some time—it's such a beautiful old place—but I really don't think it would be a good idea to do either of those things right now. Besides, my mother's expecting me to go straight to their house. So…I'd like to head right to to my mother's, if that's all right with you?'

'That's fine. No problem.'

'Thanks. We generally do a stack of baking this time of year and finish the day with decorating the tree. I think she's expecting Callum to drop by later on, too.'

'Ah.' His expression sobered. 'Then I expect you have quite a bit of catching up to do. I know he finished his university course about eighteen months ago…I saw the announcement of his honours degree in horticulture in your local paper. I have it sent over so that I can keep up with what's going on. But then I heard he'd taken a job with one of the National Trust gardens so I don't suppose you see an awful lot of him these days?'

She frowned. 'How did you hear that—about his job, I mean?'

'Anna mentioned it. She still has friends in the village who pass her snippets of news from time to time.'

'Oh, I see.' She nodded. 'Yes, he's away quite a bit. He comes back sometimes for the weekend, and of course at holiday times. The rest of the time he stays at his flat down in Essex.'

'Another man with itchy feet, then?' He sent her a considering glance. 'Anna was never sure that Callum would stay in the village, even when he qualified, and she was right, wasn't she? And maybe it was the fact that he was planning to go off to university that sparked her decision to break off with him—don't you think that's a strong possibility?'

'That's not what Callum thought, or most of the village, by all accounts. All anyone could see was that you and she were growing closer, and Millie Rossiter, the postie, saw you with your arms around her on more than one occasion.' She gave him a long look. 'So, no, I don't think that was it at all. I think she went off with you because she fell for you, big time. And we were left to pick up the pieces when Callum's world collapsed around him.'

His mouth made a rueful quirk. 'Well, I'm

sorry about that. But Anna made her own decision to leave. I was heading for Cheshire to take up a new job, and she wanted to come with me.'

She gave him a sceptical look. 'There's really no point in you trying to tell me that you had nothing to do with it. I'm siding with the rest of the villagers on this one.'

He smiled wryly. 'Yes, I thought you might.' He drove by the village green, through the small shopping centre that was the hub of community life and, after a while, turned into a leafy lane bordered by a scattering of houses. They stopped at Jasmine's cottage to drop off her case and then headed west towards the park.

Her parents lived in a large house at the end of the park road. Ben cut the engine and slid out from the driver's seat, going to stand in front of the house, looking around.

Jasmine joined him. She loved this house. It was where she and her brother had grown up, cherished by the love of both parents, and she wondered how Ben must feel, having missed out on all that. His father had always been a solitary man for the most part, immersing himself in his work, not sure how to deal with the infant son who turned to him for love and wanted so much more of his attention than he was able to give.

She looked at the rambling building, the front walls covered with neatly trimmed ivy. The front garden had a perfect, bowling-green lawn, her father's pride and joy, though now it was dotted here and there with clumps of melting snow. There were shrubs all around, firethorn, glowing with bright red berries, and berberis, showing off its rich, bronze leaves. Yellow wall-flowers peeped out from the borders.

The house was solidly built from local stone. The ground-floor rooms were used for the most part as a surgery and waiting room, but the large lounge and kitchen were kept separate from them. Upstairs, there were three bedrooms, a bathroom and a study.

Her mother must have seen them arrive, because she opened the door to them now and welcomed Jasmine with a hug. 'Thank goodness you made it home,' she said. 'I was afraid you'd be stuck in the snow for days.'

'I probably would have been, if it hadn't been for Ben.' Jasmine turned and waved Ben forward to meet her mother. 'He rescued me from the snowdrift and when I told him I needed to get back here to decorate the tree, he offered to drive me home.'

'Well, thank you for that, Ben,' her mother said, giving him a quick, but faintly cautious smile. Her green eyes were a little troubled, and she took a moment to brush back a lock of chestnut hair, tucking it behind her ear. Jasmine guessed she was debating how best to handle the situation. 'Would you like to come in and have a drink of something to warm you up?'

'No, thanks all the same, Helen. It's good of you to offer, but I have to go over to the manor, and then I've some arrangements to make at Mill House.'

'Oh, I see. Some other time, then, perhaps?' Jasmine wasn't sure whether she detected a hint of relief in her mother's acknowledging smile.

She liked Ben well enough, she guessed, but Callum would be horrified to know that his parents had welcomed him into their house, and her mother had to be conscious of that.

'Thanks again for bringing me home, Ben,' Jasmine told him, and he nodded.

She watched as he walked to his car. He wouldn't have missed her mother's hesitation, but wasn't one to let his feelings show. His stride was confident, his back straight, but she couldn't help wondering how he would fare with his father. She wished she could be at his side to lend him moral support...but, then, Ben didn't need anyone's help. He was his own man. He did what he felt to be right, no matter what the circumstances, and meeting his father after all this time was just one more challenge he had to face.

'I wasn't sure what time you would get here,' her mother said, 'so I started on the baking. I'm doing mince pies for the freezer and I've made a start on the Christmas pudding. Do you want to help? You could make your lovely fruit loaf, if you like. You know how much we love to have it for tea on Christmas Day. I have everything you need…flour, yeast, fruit, spices, and so on.'

She walked along the hallway to the kitchen, and Jasmine followed. 'I just have to put the covers on the Christmas pudding,' her mother added, 'and then it's all set to go in the pan of water. I'd better get moving—it has to cook for eight hours…' She rolled her eyes. 'I shall have to set the timer to remind me to keep topping up the water.'

'I thought I could smell delicious things coming from the kitchen.' Jasmine smiled. She loved her mother's Christmas traditions, the baking sessions where she would prepare everything possible ahead of the big day.

'I've made a pot of tea, and there's pizza and salad for lunch later on. Your father's off on his rounds, so he won't be back for a while.' Her mother was already bringing out cups and saucers, and Jasmine went to wash her hands at the sink. Then she put on an apron and readied herself to start cooking.

'So what does Ben have to say for himself?' her mother asked as they carefully kneaded dough. 'Apart from the fact that he's planning on coming home? Is he still with Anna?'

Jasmine made a face. 'I'm not sure exactly what the situation is. I'm certain he's still seeing her, and she stays at his place sometimes, but I don't think it's a full-on relationship any more. She has a little boy, four years old, and I think he feels that he has to take care of them.'

'Good heavens.' Her mother's eyes widened and she stopped what she was doing, lifting her hands away from the dough. 'I suppose the child must be his?' She frowned. 'He has to be, given that they've been away from here for five years. That's going to be a bitter blow for Callum, isn't it?'

'What's going to be a bitter blow for me?' The male voice startled both women, and they turned to see Callum walk into the kitchen. He must have let himself in by the front door, and now he dropped a couple of holdalls onto the floor and went to put his arms around his mother. Tall and strong bodied, his embrace engulfed her. 'It's good to see you again, Mum,' he said, his grey eyes filled with affection. 'You too, Jass,' he added, coming to give her a quick hug.

'We weren't expecting you till later,' Helen said, wiping her hands on a tea towel.

'I know, but I've worked the weekend, filling in for a colleague, and the boss gave me the nod to finish early. I have time off until Christmas now, so I've brought a big case.'

'And a load of washing, too, by the looks of things.' His mother smiled as she noted one of the bulging bags.

He gave a sheepish grin. 'So what's this thing I'm not going to like?' he asked, checking the teapot to see if it was hot and then reaching for a cup. 'Have you gone and let my room out to a stranger while I've been away? Don't tell me you're casting your only son out onto the street?'

'Oh, now, there's an idea.' Helen put on a thoughtful expression. 'Letting your room out…that could turn out to be quite a lucrative proposition, couldn't it? Why didn't I think of that?' Her mouth twitched at the corners.

Callum made a wry face, and turned to Jasmine. 'Are you going to tell me what's going on? What's happening?' He swallowed his tea like a man escaping from a desert.

'We were just saying that Ben Radcliffe's coming back to live in the village,' she told him. She wasn't sure how wise it would be to mention Anna in the same breath, let alone tell him about her son. 'He'll be living at Mill House and working with the rescue services.'

Callum's face became shuttered. 'How do you know that?'

She sent him a quick, appraising look. It was difficult to know how he would react after all this time, but the signs so far weren't good. 'We met up on the last day of my course, and then he helped me out when my car was stuck in a snowdrift. He told me he plans to work here for a couple of months, based at Wellbeck Hospital.'

'I see.' He put down his cup and seemed to

be waiting for the information to sink in. After a moment or two, he said flatly, 'At least I'm forewarned. I should be able to steer clear of him.'

He pulled out a chair and sat down at the table. 'Is there any news of Anna? How's she doing? I've heard bits and pieces over the years from her friends. She's kept up with the baking, so I'm told. And they say she's still with Ben…or, at least, still close to him.'

Jasmine looked to her mother for help. What was she to say? Anna's friends had obviously kept quiet about the child. Her mother looked apprehensive, but lifted her hands in an expansive, resigned gesture that Jasmine took as a signal to go ahead.

'She's been running her own specialty catering business from home—making cakes, biscuits and the like.' She frowned. 'But there is something else you should know…she has a child, a little boy.'

Callum's swift intake of breath was audible. He was silent for a while, his dark head bent, and then he said in a taut voice, 'I suppose it was inevitable. He was always a charmer, that one, so why should Anna be the exception to the rule?'

Jasmine laid a gentle hand on his shoulder. 'I'm sorry, Callum. None of us would have wanted you to come home to this. Are you going to be all right?'

He straightened. 'Of course. I've had five years to get her out of my system, haven't I? I'll be fine.'

His glance roamed over his holdalls. 'Maybe I'll go and take these upstairs,' he suggested, looking towards their mother. 'Is it all right if I put the laundry in the wash bin? I'd quite like to have the blue shirt ready for tomorrow's Christmas dance, if that's okay? I thought I'd better make my presence felt, and give the local girls a run for their money.'

Helen gave a motherly smile. 'That's my boy, practical as ever. Of course it's all right. I'll put your things in the washer overnight.'

He stood up and gave her a quick kiss. 'Thanks, Mum. You're an angel.'

They watched as he left the room, and for a while neither of them spoke. They knew his words about the village Christmas dance were pure bravado, and it was clear he wanted to be alone for a while.

Jasmine kept her thoughts to herself and continued to knead the dough for a minute or two before shaping it into a crescent.

'I'd forgotten about the village social evening,' she said a moment or two later. 'I suppose everyone will be there.'

'Everyone except Stuart Radcliffe, I imagine. He rarely attends that sort of thing.' Her mother's gaze was far away. 'I can't help feeling sorry for that man, somehow. I know he seems austere in his attitude, and he can be brusque in the extreme sometimes, but how can we know what goes on inside his head? He must be a deeply troubled man, but he keeps it all locked up inside, and that can't be good for him, can it?'

'No, probably not.' Jasmine's thoughts swivelled to Ben. How was his meeting with his father going? And had he managed to find out anything more about his illness? Would he be able to do anything to help him?

By the following day, Sunday, the sun's rays had seen off the last of the snow. Everything in the garden looked newly washed and clean, and by the end of the day Jasmine looked about her cottage, pleased that everything in there was equally fresh and sparkling. Perhaps her feverish burst of house cleaning had to do with the fact that Ben was back home after all these years, and she needed a way of clearing him from her mind. The only way she knew how to do that was to keep busy.

At around half past six that evening, she was looking through her wardrobe, trying to decide what to wear for the dance. Something chic and sophisticated, perhaps, or should she go for floaty and feminine...or maybe a glitzy party dress? She couldn't decide, and as she was checking her closet once more, the doorbell rang downstairs.

She abandoned her search and went to answer the door. Ben stood on her porch, leaning negligently against the wooden post, eyeing the winter flowering jasmine that scrambled over the trellis around her door. Looking at him, her heart missed a beat. He was dressed in an immaculate dark grey suit, cut from fine-quality material, and his shirt was a soft dove-grey, enlivened by a silk tie in gentle tones of grey and blue. He looked truly impressive and her whole body responded to his presence with a surge of unbidden yearning.

'I was beginning to think you weren't going to answer,' he said, his tone dry. 'Did you realise it was me and decide to wait till I went away?' He studied her, a glimmer of amusement in his eyes. 'Obviously, I wasn't going to do that.'

She pulled herself together. 'I was trying to decide what to wear to the Christmas dance this evening,' she murmured, ushering him inside the cottage. She showed him into her small kitchen and switched on the coffee machine. 'You get girls wearing all sorts of outfits to these things, and I'm having trouble making up my mind.'

'You'd look good whatever you wear,' he murmured, his gaze lingering on her soft, feminine curves.

She tried not to respond to his flirtatious manner, but her pulse began to beat a little faster and, when she tried to speak, her voice sounded husky to her ears.

'Perhaps you'd like to sit down?' She waved him to a seat by the pine table. 'I expect you'd like a cup of coffee.' She set out cups and then asked casually, 'Are you planning on going to the dance?'

He nodded. 'I thought it might be a good opportunity to speak to one or two business contacts. I need to clear up some issues over the building work I'm having done…and, besides, I have to attend because the vicar asked me to run the raffle. He collared me in the street yesterday and had me in a corner, so I really couldn't come up with an excuse. That was after he wrung a raffle donation out of me… I promised a couple of bottles of champagne from the cellar at the mill, along with an iced Christmas cake and a hamper. He seemed quite pleased overall.'

'I should imagine he would be, at that.'

'Anyway,' he said, 'I wondered if you'd like to go with me? I know it's a bit late to ask, but I've had a lot to sort out since I arrived back here. We could drive down there, if you like. It's a fair walk from here, and it looks as though it's going to be a cold night.' He paused, a frown crossing his brow. 'Unless, of course, you already have a date?'

'I don't. I was planning on being a wallflower at the back of the hall.'

He laughed. 'That would never happen. I've seen the way the local men eye you up. They must have asked and you refused.'

'Ah, well, I wasn't sure I'd be able to make it with my shift patterns. As it happens, though, I don't have to be back at work till Tuesday…at least by then I should have my car back.'

'So, will you come with me? Is it a date?'

'I… Yes, I'll come with you.' Her gaze was troubled. 'But let's not think of it as a date, shall we?' She ran her tongue over dry lips. 'You know, this isn't easy for me. I have to think about Callum. He'll be there, and I don't want to do anything that will cause him any grief.'

He gave her a look that was half cynical, half resigned. 'Don't you think it's time Callum got over it and moved on? You can't live your life forever concerning yourself with what Callum thinks and feels. Shouldn't you be following your own instincts?'

She gave a short laugh. 'If I did that, I'd have taken to my heels whenever you came within shouting distance. You don't have the best reputation in the world, Ben…a girl would have to be out of her mind to take your soft words to heart. And as to Callum, he's my brother, my family—but you wouldn't know about that kind of loyalty, would you? You never had a close family, so you don't understand about the ties that bind.' She shook her head, causing the chestnut waves to quiver. 'I don't blame you for that. I just think it's sad, that's all.' She poured the coffee and pushed a cup towards him.

He pressed a hand to his heart and put on a pained expression. 'I think I'm stung by all that you've just said. I may not have brothers and sisters, or any kind of close family unit, but that doesn't mean I don't understand what it is to care for someone. I loved my grandmother, and I miss her terribly. I was always fiercely loyal to her…she was like a mother to me. And even though my father and I have a difficult relationship, I do care about him. I just wish that I could find some way to break through the barriers he puts up.'

She sat down at the table and looked at him, her green eyes showing her concern. 'Did things not go well yesterday between you?'

'Not really.' He tested the heat of the coffee against his lips and sipped slowly. 'It's strange, isn't it, how much our parents' opinion matters? Even when we're grown men and women, successful in whatever we do, we need to know that we have that ultimate approval.'

He rested his cup on the saucer. 'I'm not going to get it, of course, because my father's pride demands that I follow his beliefs and traditions, and any deviation from that is taken as an insult.' He gave a negligent shrug. 'It doesn't really matter, because I've made my own way in life, and I can get by easily enough without him or his blessing, but it would have been good to break through that stubborn streak of his and find some way of reaching a new rapport.' He sighed. 'It's not to be, though.'

She frowned. 'I'm sorry. I hoped you and he might be able to patch things up. Perhaps his illness makes it more difficult for him to do that? People who are ill might tend to be tetchy or even unreasonable sometimes.'

'I doubt that's his problem, but you're right, he's not at all well, and it doesn't help.'

'How bad is it?'

He pulled in a deep breath. 'Bad enough. I think his high blood pressure is beginning to have an effect on his kidneys, and if he carries on the way he is, there could be some permanent damage. He's not taking his condition seriously enough, in my opinion. He says he missed his last monitoring session at the blood-pressure clinic, and he hasn't been back to his GP—your father—for a while. Apparently he doesn't have an appointment with the consultant for another three months, but I think he needs to go sooner.'

'I'm guessing he wouldn't let you examine him, so how do you know all this?'

'I noticed that his ankles were swollen, as well as his hands, and he seemed quite breathless, so there's probably a build-up of fluid on his lungs as well. He's taking ACE inhibitors to lower his blood pressure, along with beta blockers to regulate the heartbeat, but he needs to take a diuretic as well.' He grimaced. 'I tried to tell him that he needs to cut down on salt and eat a healthy diet, but I'm afraid my advice didn't go down too well.'

'You mean he didn't listen?'

He made a wry face. 'Oh, he listened. He just said that if he needed help he was perfectly capable of going to see his own doctor and he didn't need any input from me. In other words, mind my own business.'

'Oh, dear.' She could understand Ben's frustration. No matter what he said or did, there was no moving his father. He had taken up an inflexible stance, and Ben must feel as though he was banging his head against a wall. It was to his credit that he kept on trying. 'For what it's worth, I think you're doing the right thing by keeping the lines of communication open. I don't see how you can do any more, given the way he is.'

She was thoughtful for a moment. 'Would it be worth my asking my father to call him in to the surgery for a check-up…say that he's been going through his records and feels it's time for a routine examination, given his blood-pressure results and the fact that he missed his last appointment?'

He nodded. 'I'm sure that would be a great start. I know he respects your father. He might be able to get him to see sense.'

'I'll do that, then. He'll be at the dance tonight, so I'll try to find an opportunity to have a word with him about it.'

'Thanks.' His glance trailed over her. 'So, aren't we supposed to be there in about half an hour?'

She looked at the clock. 'Oh, heavens,' she said. 'Look at the time… And I'm still sitting here, when I should be getting ready.' She stood up and headed towards the door. Turning around, she said, 'Help yourself to more coffee. Read the paper. Just…just amuse yourself for half an hour or so, while I get ready.'

'Half an hour, when you're already perfection?' He raised a dark brow. 'Totally unnecessary but, yes, don't worry about me. I'll be fine down here.'

She shot off up the stairs and went back to checking her closet. Ben would be perfectly all right, hanging around downstairs, wouldn't he? If he hadn't turned up on her doorstep, she would be more than ready by now.

Some time later, she peered at her image in

the mirror. Her dress was made of a soft, silky fabric, with thin shoulder straps and a bodice that was decorated with beads. The skirt swirled gently around her knees as she walked. She had brushed her hair until it gleamed, leaving it to fall over her shoulders, and she used a light touch with her make-up, adding soft colour to her cheeks.

Satisfied that she was ready at last, she picked up her bag and went downstairs.

'Wow.' Ben's eyes widened. He sat there, looking at her and not saying another word, as though he was utterly speechless, but at the same time his gaze wandered over her, taking in every detail of her appearance.

She waited, not knowing quite how to respond, and then he added softly, 'You take my breath away. You're stunning, Jassie, absolutely stunning.'

It gave her a warm feeling inside, knowing that he liked the way she looked, and that sense of well-being stayed with her all the way to the village hall where the dance was being held.

Only then, as she walked through the door, did she wonder how she was going to deal with the issue of her brother.

The evening was already in full swing, with the local band playing popular music. The dance floor was crowded, and at one side of the room people were helping themselves to a finger buffet. The hall was decorated with glittering streamers of red and gold, and there were garlands of holly and berries to either side of the platform where the band was performing.

'Perhaps we should go and look for Callum,' Ben said, as though his mind was running along the same groove as hers. 'That way, hopefully, your evening won't be spoiled with worrying about his reaction.'

She nodded. 'He's over by the bar. I'll go and have a word with him.' She had thought Ben might stay behind and talk to one or two friends who were milling about near the buffet table, but instead he came with her.

'How are things with you, Callum?' he asked, as they approached. Ben went to stand next to her brother, and ordered drinks from the barman, turning to Jasmine to find out what she wanted.

Callum stiffened. 'I'd say I was fine until you came along,' he said, his voice taut. 'What happened? Did you decide to come back and wreak more havoc? From what I've been hearing this evening, you're all set to build a hotel on the land next to the mill. That hasn't gone down well with the bed-and-breakfast proprietors around here, I can tell you.'

Ben handed Jasmine a glass of red wine. 'Well, you'll be able to tell your friends that I'm not planning on building a hotel, so that's one worry out of the way, isn't it?' He looked at Callum's empty glass. 'Can I buy you a drink?'

Callum shook his head. 'No, thanks. I'll buy my own.' He nodded towards the barman to fill up his glass again. 'So where's Anna these days? Have you left her and moved on to my sister?' He sent Jasmine a piercing glance so that she shifted uncomfortably and tried to look him in the eye without flinching.

'Not at all,' Ben said smoothly. 'Anna will be coming back to Woodsley shortly. She's going to be staying for a while…a couple of months, at least…so I imagine you and she will have a chance to become reacquainted.'

Jasmine gave a soft intake of breath. Anna was coming back here?

Callum's expression turned to a glower. 'I think I've said all that I want to say to you.' He looked at Jasmine. 'I hope you know what you're doing.'

'Ben helped me out a lot over the last couple of days,' she told him. 'I'm very grateful to him. It doesn't mean I'm planning on starting a full-blooded affair. Callum, you're my brother, and I love you, but you have to try to get over the past and think about the future. Anna played as much a part in your break-up as Ben did. And maybe you had a role to play, too.'

'And maybe you need to think a bit more carefully about who you're messing with. He's not some country boy who made an honest mistake.

He's broken a lot of hearts around here and then casually walked away without looking back.'

'I doubt he was to blame on all counts. Anyway, I'm all grown up now, Callum. You don't need to watch out for me.' She said it convincingly enough, but his words had hit a little too close to home, and now she moved away from the bar, leaving her brother and Ben to continue their frosty exchange. 'I'm going to talk to friends for a while,' she murmured. She glanced at Ben. 'Why don't you go and talk to the people you wanted to see? I'll be over the other side of the room if you come looking for me.'

She didn't want to fall out with either of them. This was a Christmas dance, an annual event where villagers came in good spirits and looked forward to the coming festivities. It would have been good to find a little Christmas cheer coming her way, but it looked as though it wasn't to be.

She went to find her parents and talked to them for a while, sipping her wine and feeling its warmth creep through the whole of her body.

It occurred to her that she ought to find something to eat before the alcohol had the better of her.

'I'll get my receptionist to give Stuart a ring,' her father said. 'It sounds as though he needs his medication updated.'

'Thanks, Dad. I appreciate it.'

After a while, friends came to join in the conversation, and Jasmine talked to them for a few minutes before going to help herself to hors d'oeuvres and a glass of mulled wine from a serving bowl on the buffet table. Then she joined her friends on the dance floor, moving in time to the beat of the music, letting the throbbing notes of the guitars and keyboard fill her soul.

Ben came in search of her when she was taking a break, talking to a young man who worked at the local garage. He slid an arm around her shoulders, a possessive, deliberate action, and clearly her companion took that as a hint to leave. He made a rueful face and went to find another girl to chat up.

'Sorry to leave you to your own devices for so long,' Ben said. 'I managed to iron out a few problems with the local builders and the man from the planning department. No such luck with your brother, though. I hoped I might be able to reason with him, but I had about as much success as I did with my father. I'd say your brother and I have reached a mutual stand-off. I don't see any way the situation can be easily resolved, so we may as well leave things alone for now.'

'You're probably right. Callum's been mulling things over all this time, so he isn't going to change his attitude overnight.'

'No, I suppose not.' He looked at her, his gaze moving down to her strappy silver shoes. 'It would be a crime not to give those a full outing, don't you think? Shall we dance?' He laid a hand on the small of her back and drew her onto the dance floor.

They joined the throng of people twisting and turning and generally moving to the rhythm of the music in any way they could, and the floor was so crowded that they were frequently jostled together. Laughing, Ben caught hold of her and held her close, pulling her gently to him. 'We could make our own special dance,' he murmured, his voice rough edged. He lowered his head so that his cheek softly grazed hers. 'Just the two of us, one that lasts the whole night long.'

His words brought a swift surge of heat to race through her entire body, and even as her hands discovered his hard rib cage, she knew that she ought to resist him. She was powerless, though, unable and unwilling to pull back from his tender embrace. He made her feel that above all she was a sensual being, and her body craved his touch.

And he was happy enough to oblige. His hand was lightly stroking the small of her back, drawing her ever nearer to him, so that her feminine curves were moulded to him and his thighs lightly brushed hers.

She was dizzy with sensation. The music throbbed in her head and all she wanted was for him to go on holding her like this for ever. She didn't even notice that he had carefully led her to a far corner of the room, where the lights were dim and they were shielded from prying eyes by a large Christmas tree.

It was only when she lifted her gaze to drink in his features in the soft light that she realised they were virtually alone in this little island of tranquillity. It was as though the outside world didn't exist. The people on the other side of the tree were oblivious to them and all that mattered was that she was here with him. His arms were around her and his hands were stroking her, smoothing over the curve of her hips, urging her ever closer to him.

The music pounded in her head, reaching a crescendo, an explosion of sound, and a brief moment of sanity intervened. 'I'm not sure how this fits in with your idea of good behaviour,' she said huskily. 'I have too much to lose, letting you work your magic on me, and you must know that I'm a little light-headed from the wine, or I wouldn't have let you get this far.'

He nuzzled her cheek with his lips, and murmured softly, 'There's no problem that I can see, Jassie. You only have to look up to see that.' He placed a curled finger lightly beneath her chin and tilted her head upwards.

A sprig of mistletoe hovered over them, the pale berries a stark contrast to the dark, green leaves. 'You see?' he said, his voice a coaxing rumble against her cheek. 'Mistletoe is for lovers… And I'd love more than anything to fulfil its promise…to kiss you and make you mine, just for one moment.'

He didn't wait for her to answer and, if the truth were known, she couldn't have spoken at all right then. The mistletoe gleamed faintly above them, and she knew that what she wanted more than anything was for him to kiss her, a long, sweet and thorough kiss…and as if he had read her mind, that's exactly what he did. His lips lightly stroked hers, trailing fire where they touched, teasing them apart, and then he deepened the kiss, softly demanding, coaxing a response that she gave only too willingly.

Her fingers slid over his chest, gliding upwards to trace the line of his shoulders and his throat. She wanted him, she loved the feel of him, and the only thing that stood between them was the fact that they were in a room full of people.

That thought had a sobering effect on her. Cautiously, she eased her hands away from him and reluctantly drew back. 'This is the wrong place,' she whispered. 'The wrong time.'

'And the wrong man.' Her brother's clipped voice reached her through the haze of desire and alcohol. Slowly, she turned to face him, conscious that Ben had drawn back from her but still kept an arm around her waist.

'Callum,' she said shakily, 'what are you doing here? I mean, why are you saying this to me?' Her words were confused, and that was because her mind was struggling to take in what was going on.

'I'm warning you that you're playing with fire,' he said. 'You know how he manages to seduce every woman in sight. Haven't you learned anything? He has time on his hands and you just happen to be available.'

His glance flicked to Ben. 'I came to tell you that there's a phone call for you. Apparently, Anna's been trying to get in touch with you, but it seems you were too busy paying attention to my sister to answer your mobile. Or, who knows, maybe you switched it off so that you could concentrate better. She managed to get through to one of her friends instead. Apparently she needs you to call her urgently.'

Ben frowned. 'Thanks, Callum. Thanks for letting me know. I'll give her a call right now.'

Callum sent Jasmine a quick, appraising glance. 'I thought better of you. Are you going to throw away your integrity for the sake of a brief fling with the likes of him? I don't know you any more.'

Jasmine stared at him. Callum had every right to be annoyed with her. Wasn't he simply telling her what she already knew?

All at once she was distressed, conscious that she had let her brother down. She couldn't think what had possessed her. She knew that all the things he said were true, and yet once again she had allowed herself to be coaxed into Ben's arms. Would she never learn?

CHAPTER SIX

'I CAN'T stop more than five minutes, Mum, because I'm on my way to work, but I've brought the holly that you wanted… And there's a bottle of whisky for Dad, as a thank you for taking me to collect my car.' Jasmine placed a carrier bag on the kitchen worktop. 'There are some lovely red berries on the sprigs—I had to rescue them because the redwings and fieldfares were having themselves a feast and soon there would have been none left.'

Callum was eating breakfast at the table to one side of the room and she sent him a quick smile, but he merely glanced her way, stony faced, and said nothing.

It hurt that he ignored her, but she tried to tell herself that he would come around eventually. Okay, so she'd kissed Ben…was that really such a dreadful crime? She'd taken herself to task over this far more than Callum could ever have done. In part she could blame the alcohol, but for the rest…Ben had found his way into her heart and now she was torn in two.

'Thanks, Jasmine,' her mother said. 'I was hoping you would remember. I've always admired that lovely holly bush at the end of your garden. As to the whisky, you didn't need to do that—but I'm sure your father will appreciate it very much.'

She inspected the contents of the bag, and Jasmine added, 'There are some fir cones in there, too, that I picked up from the woods a while back. Do you have the gold and silver spray paint that you need?'

Her mother nodded. 'I do. I'll get on with making the Christmas wreath for the door just as soon as I can find a spare minute. With one thing and another, shopping, baking and so on, on top of working, it's all go just now.' She carefully emptied out the sprigs of holly and spread them on the worktop. 'I've enough here to make one for you, too, if you like.'

Jasmine nodded. 'I'd love that, thanks. It's a good thing you only work part-time nowadays, isn't it?' she commented with a smile. 'And maybe it's just as well that there aren't too many expectant mothers in the village due to give birth any time soon, otherwise you and Dad could be out delivering babies on Christmas Day.'

'That's true. But you can never tell with babies, can you? They often turn up off schedule and catch us all hopping.'

'And then everyone's glad to have you around to smooth the process along.' She studied her mother. 'You love your job, don't you?'

Helen nodded. 'There's something very satis-fying about bringing babies into the world.' She glanced at Jasmine. 'I half expected you to go in for that line of work, but instead you chose A and E. For myself, I'm not sure I could cope with it long term.'

'No, it isn't to everyone's taste, I grant you.

But my role's changing from today. The boss rang to confirm it—I'm to be on call with the rescue services, and it's been written into my contract that I go along as a first responder with the team. My only problem is that Ben is likely to be working with me, both at the hospital and with the rescue team. I'm just not quite sure how the land lies there. He's taken on a temporary job as locum registrar, but what happens after his two-month stint, I'm not sure. Perhaps he'll get wanderlust again. Quite how that will affect his work with the rescue services is anybody's guess.' And how would she feel if he decided to leave the village once more? She was fool-hardy to even contemplate getting involved with Ben.

'Two months is the same length of time he said Anna would be staying in Woodsley,' Callum put in. His stare was hard and unflinching. 'Did you know that she'll be staying at Mill House for all that time?'

Jasmine ran the tip of her tongue over her lips. 'No, I didn't.' The fact that Anna would be living with Ben was definitely unsettling. It made her wonder if she really knew Ben at all. 'He doesn't tell me everything that's going on in his life. I still don't know what prompted Anna's call to him the other night. He left the village hall and went straight back to Cheshire.'

'Doesn't that tell you something about what's going on with him? How many men do you know who would drop everything to be at a woman's side?' He scowled. 'You're just an interlude to him, Jass…a pleasant way of passing the time.'

Jasmine pulled in a shuddery breath. 'I don't know about that. You may be right, but neither of us knows what really goes on in his mind, do we?'

'Maybe not, but I do know that Anna's going into hospital—Wellbeck. One of her friends told me that Anna had a message to say her appointment has been brought forward. She said that Ben will be bringing her over here today.' He frowned, giving Jasmine a cool look. 'Did you know about that? Do you know why she's going into hospital?'

Jasmine hesitated. 'I do…but I've been asked not to say anything. If you want to know any more about it, you'll have to go and see her at the hospital and ask her for yourself. That shouldn't be too hard, should it? I know you've tried to keep in touch with her from time to time, so it won't come as a surprise to her to know that you care. I'm sure the hospital will let you know what ward she's on and tell you about visiting times.' Wellbeck was probably the most sensible choice for her surgery, since her original consultant would be able to supervise her care…and that most likely had some part to play in Ben's decision to return home at this particular time.

He gritted his teeth. 'You're my sister. Isn't blood thicker than water? Aren't you supposed to side with me and confide in me?'

'You're my brother. Shouldn't you have trusted me to handle my own relationships and do what I think best?' she countered. 'Shouldn't you have tried to see things from my point of view? You and Anna aren't a couple any more. Why should I have to tread on eggshells because of what once went on between you? Five years have gone by and we've all changed in some way.'

Callum didn't answer. His mouth was clamped shut as he turned away from her, and he concentrated his attention on the morning paper. Jasmine clenched her fingers into small fists and tried to rid herself of her frustration. Then she glanced at her mother to see how she had been affected by their bickering.

'Perhaps you should get off to work,' her mother said. 'I hope it goes well for you. Are you going out with the rescue team today?'

'Only if there's a problem that the usual emergency services can't handle.' Jasmine picked up her bag and went to the door. 'I'll see you later,' she said, and then, after a moment's hesitation, called back, ''Bye, Callum.'

He stayed silent, and Jasmine went out to her car feeling tense and despondent.

She drove to the hospital and once she was there she tried to lose herself in her work. She was conscious that Ben might put in an appearance at any time, but she guessed he was helping Anna to settle in on her hospital ward.

Presumably the surgery had been advanced unexpectedly, and that must have upset Anna's arrangements. Who would be taking care of her little boy?

Jasmine tried to steer her mind away from such thoughts. She needed to pay full attention to her work, and in A and E everything was much as usual, except that the icy weather conditions in some parts had created havoc, and they had to deal with an unusual number of accidents due to falls.

Ben didn't arrive in the department until late afternoon and then it was to tell her that he'd just had a call out to Coniston Old Man, one of the local mountains.

'Yes, I heard about it,' she said. 'I'd like to come along, if I may—just for the experience.

I've finished here for the day and handed over my workload, so I'm ready to go.'

He nodded. 'That's fine by me. I've spent most of the afternoon working on a patient who had a complicated chest injury, but thankfully he was out of the woods before I had to ask a colleague to take over.'

'A difficult case?'

'Yes. I had to open up his chest as an emergency procedure, but his condition deteriorated and he went into cardiac arrest. ' He was already walking with her to the exit doors. 'We managed to get him back, though.'

'I'm glad.' She smiled at him. 'You must be very relieved.' She picked up her jacket from the locker room. 'So how are we getting to the meeting point?'

'I'll drive. We'll park up at Coniston village and join up with the rest of the team. From there it will be a climb taking us up close to the summit. A man fell and broke his leg, I'm told, and so the sooner we get there, the better.'

'Let's hope that whoever's with him has

thought to keep him warm. Hypothermia's one of the main hazards in these conditions, isn't it?'

'That's right.' They were already on their way out to the car park. Jasmine retrieved her mountain rescue kit from the boot of her car, and then went to sit beside Ben in the BMW.

He set the car in motion, and then glanced at her obliquely. 'I'm sorry I had to leave you so abruptly on Sunday evening.'

'That's all right,' she murmured. She didn't want to think about that evening and all the emotions it had stirred in her. 'I realise you didn't have much choice. Anna needed you, didn't she?'

He nodded. 'The surgery was brought forward because of a cancellation elsewhere, so she's being prepped for Theatre at this very moment.'

'What kind of surgery is she having?'

'An aortic valve replacement. Her own valve had only two cusps instead of three, and over the years it became more and more obstructed, so that her symptoms worsened. The cusps became stiff and calcified, so that blood couldn't circulate efficiently, and in the end she was increasingly breathless and started having chest pains. Pregnancy made things worse, and her heart rhythm became abnormal. That was when the cardiologist decided that she needed a replacement valve.' His expression was sombre. 'Anna was reluctant to go ahead with the surgery because she was afraid of what would happen to Kyle if anything went wrong.'

Jasmine felt a sudden rush of concern. 'Poor Anna. She must have been in a dreadful state. How is she bearing up?'

'Okay, I think. She's resigned to the inevitable, but I've managed to persuade her that I'll be looking after Kyle and she needn't have any worries on that score. I just want her to relax and concentrate on getting through the operation.'

Jasmine frowned. 'So where is Kyle now? Who's going to be taking care of him while you're working?'

'I've booked him in with a registered childminder in the village. If it wasn't so near Christmas he would have been at school, but the way things are, I didn't have much choice. It was a bit of a stressful situation for him, of course, because he doesn't know the woman, and he doesn't understand why his cosy little world has suddenly changed, but Carole Wainright seems to be really good with children, and her house has a warm and friendly atmosphere.'

Jasmine nodded. 'I know Carole. She's a lovely woman. I often see her collecting children from the village school. I'm sure she'll help him to settle, and there will be one or two other youngsters for him to play with.'

'I guess so. It's just difficult initially. We were hoping that we would have more time to explain things to him, but we hadn't expected the date of surgery to be brought forward.' Ben turned the car onto the road to Coniston village, and already Jasmine could see Coniston Old Man looming up ahead of them. The topmost slopes were covered in snow, but lower down it was still green and inviting to any would-be climbers.

Ben sent her another sideways glance. 'I was worried about Callum's attitude towards you the other night. Did you manage to smooth things over with him, or is he still upset?'

She made a wry face. 'He's still angry with me. I don't think that's going to change any time soon. I think the trouble is he still loves Anna. I know he's written to her occasionally and tried to talk to her on the phone, but although she was pleasant to him and wanted to know how he was getting on at university and so on, she's never given him any sign that she wants to get back with him.'

She saw Ben's brooding expression and added in a quiet voice, 'I realise you might not like the fact that they kept in touch, but I have to think of my brother in this. Anna was his childhood sweetheart, and it seems to be a love he's never fully recovered from.'

'He has only himself to blame. I'm sure if he'd paid her more attention in the first place she would never have left him. He was too busy making his career plans to think about what was going on in Anna's life.'

Her mouth made a cynical twist. 'Well, you were quick enough off the mark, stepping into the breach, weren't you? She was vulnerable, and you took advantage of that. You paid attention to her when Callum was getting all fired up about going off to university. If you had done the decent thing and backed off, they might still be together.'

His jaw set in a rigid line. 'But they aren't, and I don't see any point in going over old ground.' He swung the car into the car park and Jasmine looked around to see the rescue team assembling by the exit.

'We'll make our way towards the beck,' the leader said when they joined the group a moment or two later, 'and then aim for a brisk climb. It shouldn't be too difficult, but it gets pretty steep the higher you go, and it can be gruelling, so be prepared.'

As soon as the whole team had gathered, they set off. Jasmine looked around at the houses in the area, built with stone and slate from the mountain. It was a pretty village, and later, as they started their climb and came by a stone bridge, she paused for a moment to take in the full beauty of the area. She saw verdant slopes and rocky outcrops, along with tumbling waterfalls and fast-running streams. Here and there she spotted deer grazing, and occasionally a glimpse of a squirrel darting between the trees.

Higher up they came across old mine workings and disused tunnels, and in some places there were rusty remnants of copper mining.

'Just a little further and we should reach Low Water,' Ben said, coming alongside her. 'Our patient is just a short distance from there.'

'I hope he's doing all right,' she murmured. 'Having a broken leg up here must be pretty horrendous.'

'True. Let's hope there's nothing desperately serious to warrant an emergency evacuation, but if there is, we can at least make him more comfortable. The journey down here with a stretcher is going to be a tough one.'

He was right about that. The gradient up here was steep, and she was glad she wouldn't be the one carrying the man downhill.

Low Water was beautiful, a stretch of water that was half-frozen right now on the surface, and dark green-blue in colour.

They trekked on for a few more minutes, and at last they reached their destination. The injured man was in obvious pain, pale faced, his lips taking on a bluish tinge, and even though his companions had tried to shield him from the cold by wrapping him in waterproofs, he was chilled to the bone.

Ben quickly examined him, but it was clear from the way his leg was distorted and shorter than the other one that it was broken.

'I'll give you something for the pain, Simon,' Ben said, 'and we'll make you as comfortable as we can by splinting the leg. The bones need to be realigned, but we can't do that here. It will have to wait till you reach the hospital. They'll give you an anaesthetic and do it in Theatre.'

'Something for the pain sounds good,' Simon answered, his mouth making a taut line. He began to shiver, and the members of the rescue team came forward with blankets. Others started to ready the stretcher and casualty bag that would encase the patient to provide warmth and protection.

Ben gave Simon a painkilling injection and Jasmine checked his blood pressure and listened to his heart while the injection took effect.

'At least it isn't an open fracture, so that's one less thing to worry about,' Ben remarked.

He turned to Jasmine and said in a low voice, 'I'm worried about internal bleeding. His heart is racing, and his blood pressure's falling, so there's a distinct possibility that he could go into shock. I'm going to set up an intravenous line to try to counteract any blood loss, but I think we should contact the air ambulance to see if there's any chance they can get him to hospital quicker than we can. The longer we delay, the greater the danger of neurological damage.'

'I'll call them,' Jasmine said, and started to dial the number. 'The helicopter will be here in about ten minutes,' she told him a moment or two later. 'It'll have to be a winch rescue because there's no safe place to land.'

'Okay. Let's get him splinted and wrapped up.'

She helped Ben to put the splints in place, and when they were satisfied that they had done everything they could for the man medically, they started to prepare for the evacuation process.

They strapped Simon into a harness and made sure that he was secured safely to the stretcher. 'It seems like only the other day that we were going through this routine,' Ben said, throwing her a quick look.

She saw the glimmer of amusement in his eyes. 'I suppose I should be thankful it won't be me going up on the line,' she said softly, turning away from their patient so that he wouldn't hear. 'At least you won't be the one going up there with him...or will you?'

He shook his head. 'There will be a doctor on board the helicopter. He'll take over from here.'

Ben checked their patient once more. 'How are you holding up?' he asked. 'Are you a bit warmer now?'

Simon nodded. 'I'm much more comfortable, thanks. I'm really grateful to all of you for going to all this trouble to take care of me. I feel such a fool. I've been climbing for years and never done anything like this.'

Ben smiled. 'It happens to lots of people, believe me. That's why we have the rescue services.'

They heard the drone of the helicopter just a short time later, and within a minute or two a man descended on a line, to land just a foot away from the stretcher.

Jasmine stood back while Ben helped the winch man fasten the ropes in place and make sure that the stretcher was secure. A moment or two later he gave the signal to the pilot and the line was winched up.

As the helicopter moved away, heading in the direction of Wellbeck Hospital, the rescue team celebrated a job well done with flasks of coffee and hot chocolate. Someone even produced pasties that he handed around. 'Can't go without sustenance on these missions,' he said. He passed drinks and food to the patient's companions. 'Pity we couldn't give your friend anything to drink to warm him up, but it was obvious he was going to need an anaesthetic fairly soon.'

'I'm sure he'll be okay now,' Ben said. 'He'll be in a cast over Christmas, but on the whole I think he's been lucky. We made good time up the mountain.'

They lingered for a few minutes, taking time to refresh themselves before they started the descent down the mountain.

Jasmine looked around and took in the view from this vantage point. From here, she could see the long sweep of Coniston Water and, further afield, the blue waters of Morecambe Bay.

'It's lovely, isn't it?' Ben came to stand with her, taking in the scenery. 'That's what makes climbing such a worthwhile exercise. It's invigorating, it keeps you fit, and in the end you're rewarded with fantastic views over the whole of the region.'

'It is. I love this whole area. I don't think I could ever leave.' She turned to him. 'You don't have that same tug of emotion, though, do you? You and Callum were both content to move away.'

'I don't know about Callum, but for me, home has to be about people. I was happy in Woodsley while my grandmother was alive, but after she had passed on, there was no reason for me to stay. My father didn't show any sign of wanting me around, and so I went where the best career prospects took me. I expect Callum is doing the same thing, although he knows that your parents will welcome him back with open arms at any time.'

The team members readied themselves for the descent, and Jasmine prepared to join them. 'So when your two months here is finished, will you be moving on again?' she asked.

'I haven't made any specific plans as yet,' he said. 'I have to think about Anna and Kyle and make sure that all's well with them. And, of course, I'd like to make my peace with my father. It would be good if we could share at least one Christmas with a special father and son relationship.'

Jasmine stayed quiet. His thoughts first and foremost were with Anna and the boy, and surely that was how it should be? Anna was vulnerable right now and needed him, and as for Kyle…Ben was clearly taking his responsibilities seriously.

The descent down the mountain was tricky, especially where the incline was steepest. Ben helped her, giving her a supporting hand, making sure that she didn't slip or stumble. She was grateful to him for that, but his touch made her sorrowfully aware of what she was missing. She was conscious the whole time that he belonged to someone else, if not in a binding sense, at least morally and ethically.

When they finally arrived back in Coniston village, she said goodbye to the members of the rescue team and slid into the passenger seat of Ben's car. 'I suppose you're going to pick up Kyle from Carole's house now, are you?' she asked.

He shook his head. 'I thought I'd stop by the hospital and check up on Anna first. The theatre nurse texted me to say that the operation was proceeding as planned, so by the time we get back she should be in the recovery room. I'd like to be there when she wakes up, and I want to make sure that she's all right.'

'Of course.' She pressed her lips together briefly. 'When she's able to talk, would you ask her if it's all right if I visit her? She and I always got along well together and I'd like to see how she's doing.'

'I will.'

He studied her, his gaze lingering on her face,

taking in the smooth line of her cheekbones, the fullness of her soft mouth. 'You know, when I get myself together over the next few days, I'll be starting work on the interior of the barn conversion. I could do with some advice on the furnishings and décor…and you're probably the ideal person to help me out with that. I've seen what you've done with the cottage, and you have a light, modern touch. Would you consider coming over to give me a hand with it?'

Jasmine's breath caught in her throat. On the surface, what he was asking was a simple favour, nothing untoward. But how could he know the dilemma he was thrusting onto her?

Working with him at the barn would bring her into close contact with him over a period of time…time when she should be doing her best to steer clear of him.

Knowing all this, why then did she hear herself saying softly, 'Yes, I could do that. I'd love to help out, in any way I can.'

CHAPTER SEVEN

JASMINE placed her hands at the back of her hips and slowly stretched, easing the stiffness in her spine. It had been a long day in A and E and her muscles were beginning to complain.

Looking around, though, at the main reception area and general thoroughfare, she was pleased with the festive appearance of the place. Staff had been busy, hanging glittering red and gold foil decorations here and there, and equally cheerful garlands festooned the reception desk. People might be feeling at a low ebb when they entered the department, but their mood was invariably lighter when they left. Of course, that was partly down to the care and attention they received from the medical staff. Everyone here was dedicated to the job.

'It looks as though you've had a tough day,'

Ben commented, coming to stand by the desk alongside her. 'Have you had a break lately?'

'Not for several hours. It's been non-stop in here, with nasty infections, strokes, fractures… you name it, we've seen it.' She grimaced, and then added, 'And talking of fractures, I checked up on Simon, who we sent here yesterday by air ambulance. I thought you'd like to know he's doing well, apparently. He's uncomfortable, obviously, but his fracture was reduced under anaesthetic, and now his leg's in a cast and the surgeon is thinking of discharging him some-time tomorrow.'

'That's great news. I was worried the situation might be worse, with internal bleeding causing problems.'

She nodded. 'Getting him here quickly helped tremendously, but I think they're keeping him in hospital for an extra day just to make sure he's making a proper recovery, but so far it's looking good.'

Ben smiled. 'I'm glad you thought to find out about him. I was planning on ringing Admissions myself, but I've been kept busy all day with several nasty traffic accident cases. At least all the injured are safe now, thankfully.'

She could see he was relieved about that. He looked weary, too, with lines of tiredness around his eyes that she hadn't noticed before, and her heart went out to him. He worked hard, she'd discovered. Even in the short time he'd been at this hospital, he'd impressed the staff with his dedication to the job and his care and attention towards the patients.

'Are you going off duty now?' She guessed from the work rota that he was on the same shift pattern as her.

'Yes. Carole will be dropping off Kyle at the hospital any minute now, and we're going up to see his mother in Intensive Care. She's going off to do some Christmas shopping afterwards, so she said it was no bother to bring him in.'

He sent her a quick glance. 'Would you like to come with me to see Anna? You'll be free in a few minutes, won't you? Unless, of course, you had other plans?'

'I'd love to come with you if she's up to having visitors. Did you mention to Anna I'd like to see her?'

'I did. She was pleased. Actually, she's doing really well. She had minimally invasive surgery, which means the surgeon made a smaller incision and she should experience less pain as a result. It's cosmetically better too, of course.'

'I'm glad things have worked out all right. I've been thinking about her all day.'

He nodded. 'Me, too.'

Just then there was a minor commotion at the main door, and a harassed Carole Wainright came into the emergency unit, towing a very fractious young boy. Her blonde hair was slightly tousled and there was faint look of tension in her demeanour.

'Don't want to come here,' the child said vehemently, his whole body stiff and resistant. 'Don't want to wait for Daddy-Ben. He'll be ages. He always takes a long time. I want to see my mum now.' He scowled. 'You can take me there. You maked me wait all day and I don't want to wait any more.'

The boy's chin jutted belligerently as though daring her to cross him, and the usually serene Carole gave a smile that was held in place by sheer willpower.

'Look, he's over there and he's ready now, see.' She shot Ben a look as if to say, *Please make it true, I'm about at the end of my tether.*

Ben moved forward to greet them. 'Hi, soldier,' he said, stooping to pick up the child and hold him securely in his arms. The boy glowered at him, and Jasmine couldn't help noticing that his features were very similar to Anna's, with that troubled, vulnerable look that she sometimes had. His neatly cut hair was a touch lighter than Ben's, but his eyes were that same shade of blue, with maybe a hint of grey.

'We're going to see your mother now, Kyle,' Ben said, soothingly. 'But you need to calm down, because she's very poorly and you must be on your best behaviour. Can you do that for me?'

Kyle nodded reluctantly, his mouth still truculent, as though the slightest thing might cause him to change his mind.

Ben turned his attention to Carole. 'Thanks for bringing him in, Carole. I really appreciate it. As to the rest…' his gaze flicked to the top of the boy's head '…I know what you've been going through. You're a saint, you know that, don't you?'

'I'm beginning to believe it.' Carole laughed. 'We tried out all sorts of toys and activities today to see if anything would help to rid him of his frustrations.' She winced. 'Do you know…he really liked the drum kit?'

Ben laughed. 'I can imagine how that must have cheered you up no end. Go off and enjoy your shopping, Carole. I've heard it's lovely in town now with the Christmas lights and the Salvation Army singing carols.'

'The stores are open till late, too, so that's a big relief. I've left my husband watching my two girls, so I can shop in peace.'

Carole left, and Jasmine tried to introduce

herself to Kyle. 'Hi, there,' she said in a cheerful tone. 'I'm Jasmine. I'm a friend of your mother, so we thought it would be nice if I went along with you and your daddy to see her.'

Kyle scrunched up his face as though he was trying to decide if that was a good or bad thing. In the end he gave up thinking about it and instead turned to look at Ben. 'You can put me down now,' he said. 'I'm not a baby. I'm four years old.'

Ben lifted his dark brows. 'Well, I do beg your pardon. How could I have forgotten that?' He gently lowered the boy to the floor. 'So, have you been having a good time at Carole's house?'

'No,' Kyle answered crossly. 'Her soppy girls kept telling me what to do…and they kept trying to take the drum off me. And then when I played the recorder instead, they tried to grab that. So I took their dollies and hid them where they couldn't find them and they *cried* and *cried*.' He rolled his eyes. 'And then they ran off shouting for Carole. And then I got into trouble when it wasn't my fault.' He was glowering again, and Jasmine hid a smile.

'Girls can be like that,' she said. 'They don't really understand how boys like to play, do they?'

He looked at her with a glimmer of interest. 'No.' Then he turned back to Ben. 'You said you'd take me to see my mum. You're not going to do any more work, are you? You always have to work, but I want to see her now.'

'Okay.' Ben nodded. 'Come on. Best foot forward.'

Puzzled, Kyle looked down at his feet. 'Which one is that?'

Ben gave it some thought, then pointed to the child's right foot. 'You can start with that one today, and maybe try the other one tomorrow.'

'Okay.'

They took the lift to the upper floor where Anna was being cared for in the intensive care unit. Jasmine glanced at Ben and said quietly, 'He calls you Daddy-Ben. That's unusual, isn't it? How did that come about?'

His mouth tilted at the corners. 'The first word he ever learned was *da-da*, and he would say it all the time. Any man who came by would be *da-da*. And then he listened to what was going on around him and would hear people calling me by my name, so after a while it sort of stuck. I became Daddy-Ben.'

By now they were approaching the unit, and Ben's attention swivelled back to the child.

'Your mother is in that room over there,' he said, pointing to a door ahead of them and looking down at Kyle as he and the boy walked, hand in hand, along the corridor. 'It might seem a little scary to you in there at first, so before we go in there I want you to explain to you what you'll see.'

Kyle nodded. 'Mummy will be in bed.'

'Yes, that's true, but there will be some pads on your mother's chest, with wires attached to them. They're connected to monitors to show how fast her heart is beating and to let the doctors know if her breathing is as it should be. There will be small tubes fitted just inside her nose to help her to breathe properly and perhaps another one to make her tummy more comfortable.' He studied the child. 'Are you okay with that so far?'

'Yes,' Kyle said on a doubtful note. His expression was solemn. 'Mummy's very poorly, isn't she?'

'She's doing all right, Kyle. She's had an operation to make her better, but it will be quite a long time before she's properly well again.'

'But she will get better?'

'Yes. If she gets plenty of rest, and everybody helps to look after her, she'll get better. But for now, as well as the wires, she has tubes coming from her chest, and from her arm, to make sure that she's comfortable and not in any pain.'

The enormity of the situation seemed to dawn on the boy at that moment, and it threatened to overwhelm him. He swallowed hard and his face crumpled a little as though he was about to cry. More than anything, Jasmine wanted to put her arms about him and hold him close, but she hesitated. She was a stranger to him and perhaps it wouldn't be right.

She needn't have worried, though. Ben drew the boy to him and wrapped an arm around his shoulders in a comforting gesture.

'I know it might seem as though your mother is helpless, Kyle,' he said, 'but, in fact, she isn't. She's really looking forward to seeing you, and she wants to know that you're settling in all right with Carole in the daytime when I'm at work. That way she can rest more easily. And the more she rests, the sooner she'll get better.' He placed a hand under the boy's chin and gently tilted his face so that he could look into his eyes. 'Do you understand?'

Kyle sniffed and rubbed his tears away. 'Yes.'

'That's my boy. I think you're very brave.' He held his hand once more. 'Okay, then. If you're ready, we'll go in.'

Ben pushed open the door, and Kyle stepped cautiously into the ward, casting a wary look around, as though afraid of what he might see.

Then he appeared to brace himself, and he walked slowly over to his mother's bedside.

He stayed there, silently watching Anna sleep, his gaze wandering fearfully over the myriad tubes, wires and monitors that surrounded her, his eyes widening. The monitors beeped and flashed, and Kyle pulled in a deep, shuddery breath. He said nothing, but stood very still, as though waiting for something.

At last, Anna's eyes fluttered open. 'Kyle, my little treasure,' she whispered, and her face lit up in a smile.

Then he moved, very gently reaching out to take her hand, and he bent his head towards her so that his cheek rested in the crook of her shoulder.

Watching him, Jasmine was suddenly immensely proud of this little boy. It seemed as though he was wise beyond his years, and even though he was upset and afraid, he had hidden all that from his mother.

She glanced at Ben. 'It was good that you spoke to him before we came in here,' she said in a low voice. 'Otherwise it would have been very scary for him. It's an awful lot for a young child to take in.'

He nodded and went to stand next to Kyle. He leaned over and kissed Anna on the forehead and on the cheek, and all at once Jasmine felt as though she was an intruder, as though she didn't belong here.

She hung back for a while, letting Ben and the boy have these precious moments with Anna, and just as she was thinking of retreating altogether, Ben turned around and beckoned her forward.

'You've a special visitor,' he told Anna. 'She's been worried about you. We've all been worried about you.'

Anna's eyes reflected her contentment as she saw Jasmine standing there. 'I'm so glad you came,' she said softly, her voice thready as a result of her weakened condition. 'It's been such a long time.'

Jasmine gave her a quick smile. 'Yes, it has.

I never expected to see you like this, though. How are you bearing up?'

'All right.' Anna's hand rested on Kyle's head, lightly stroking his hair. 'Better now that the operation's over and done with.'

'I can imagine. From here on, you should start to get your strength back, and hopefully life should be a lot easier for you. I'd no idea what you must have been going through.'

Anna's mouth made a small curve. 'That's what Callum said.' She spoke softly, as though everything was a bit of an effort, and Jasmine was afraid that she was becoming overtired.

'He's been here to see you?'

Anna nodded. 'I think he was shocked. It was a lot for him to take in.' She pressed her lips together. 'Of course, I was still a bit groggy from the anaesthetic yesterday. Tell him it's not as bad as it seems, will you?'

'I will.'

They stayed for a while longer, but it was clear that Anna's energy reserves were failing, and Ben very gently persuaded Kyle to relinquish his hold on his mother. 'We have to go now,' he said, 'so that your mother can get some sleep.'

Kyle tried to cling on, unwilling to move from Anna's bedside, but Anna said quietly, 'Do you know what I'd like, Kyle?'

The boy shook his head, his eyes wide and his expression solemn.

'I'd like to come home to a lovely Christmas tree. One that is fresh from the woods and smells of pine.' She smiled. 'I wonder if you and Daddy-Ben could find one like that for me?'

Kyle looked up at Ben, his gaze questioning, and Ben nodded. 'We could go out to the woods on Saturday and pick one out, if you like.'

The child nodded vigorously. 'Yes,' he said. 'A great big, enormous tree—this big.' He spread his arms wide open to show how wide it would be, and then looked up at the ceiling. 'And it will go right up to there.'

Ben chuckled. 'I can see we're going to have fun finding just the right one.'

They left Anna a few minutes later and headed out to the car park. Ben walked with Jasmine to her car, holding Kyle's hand so that the boy didn't dash out into the road.

'Would you like to come with us to pick out the tree?' he asked, holding open the car door for her so that she could slide into the driver's seat. 'Between the three of us, we should manage to find one that's exactly right.'

The invitation startled her, but she was pleased to be included in the outing. 'I'd like that,' she said. She looked at Kyle, who was kicking up remnants of snow from the grass verge. 'Is that all right with you?'

The boy's shoulders moved in a negligent gesture. 'Yeah, sure.'

She looked back at Ben, a smile hovering on her lips. 'I guess that's settled, then.'

She started the car's engine and waved goodbye to them, conscious of Ben's thoughtful gaze as she drove out of the car park a short time later.

It had been strange seeing him with Anna, watching his gentleness with her, the way he kissed her with such deep affection. What exactly was his relationship with her? It seemed as though they shared a loving bond, and even though Ben said their relationship was not quite the same as it once had been, he had made arrangements for Anna to stay with him at his house.

Where did that leave her, with Ben trying to steal kisses? She couldn't work out what was going on in his head. His involvement with Anna made everything even more bewildering.

And what about Kyle? He certainly seemed to love the boy in the way that a father would love his son. His whole attitude to the child was considerate and caring. She frowned. None of this made any sense and she was thoroughly confused. What was he doing, making plans to be with her while Anna lay ill in bed?

Perhaps his invitation for her to join them on Saturday had been a spur-of-the-moment thing. Maybe he wasn't thinking logically, but instead was following his instincts. Whatever the reasoning behind the suggestion, she realised that she was looking forward to spending time with him.

It snowed again over the next couple of days, and by the time Ben arrived with Kyle to pick her up at lunchtime on Saturday, the whole landscape was covered in a blanket of white. Kyle was dressed in a warm coat and trousers, with a woolly hat and Wellington boots, and he took great delight in making footprints in the virgin snow.

'I hope you're ready for this,' Ben commented, glancing at Jasmine as they settled themselves in his car. 'Kyle's in fine form today. The tree has to be exactly right, and he's intent on examining every single one in the forest from the sound of things.'

Jasmine laughed. 'So we're in for the long haul. I'll bear that in mind.'

'Carole says there's a playground at the forest,' Kyle put in eagerly, 'where you can climb on fallen down trees and swing on ropes and things. I want to do that. And I want to crawl through the tunnels. She says there are little dens and things what you can play in.' He drummed his fingers on his knees in expectation and looked out of the window to see how far they had gone along the road. 'Will we soon be there?'

'It takes about half an hour. Sit back and see if you can spot any birds' nests high up in the trees as we go along,' Ben suggested. 'There won't be any birds in them, this time of year, but you should be able to see the nests now that the branches are bare.'

Kyle began to stare intently at the passing scenery and for a while peace reigned.

'I've never been out to this forest,' Jasmine said when they finally turned into the car park. 'It sounds as though everything's geared up here for a family day out.'

'That's the general idea, I think.' He locked up the car and they set off along the path, with Kyle keeping a lookout for the playground.

'There it is,' he said, after a minute or two, giving a joyful whoop. 'I'm going over there now.' He raced away, as fast as he could go with his boots making inroads in the deep snow, leaving Jasmine and Ben to follow at their own pace.

'I don't suppose he can come to any harm around here,' Ben commented, scanning the playground. All the activities were woodland based, a children's paradise, with climbing frames and wooden structures to be explored. 'Shall we go and sit on the bench and watch him for a while?'

'Good idea.'

They cleared the snow off a nearby bench and sat together, following Kyle's progress as he embarked on his adventure.

'Have you been to see Anna recently?' Jasmine asked. 'They moved her from Intensive Care on Thursday, so that was a good sign. I've been trying to go and visit her every day, but the times vary, according to when I can get a break from work.'

'Yes, same here. I dropped by the hospital with Kyle this morning. She looks much stronger, and with a bit of luck they'll be sending her home on Monday.' He smiled. 'At least that will give me time to get the tree installed and decorated. I think it was a good idea of Anna's to give Kyle something to focus on but, then, she always knew how to handle him.'

'You don't seem to do too badly yourself.' Jasmine gazed at him, taking in his strong features, the firm angle of his jaw, his beautifully moulded mouth. He was incredibly good looking, but there was more to him than that, much more. He was also a good and capable man, one who shouldered his responsibilities, who made his own way in life and took in his stride the knocks along the way. This was a man she could love, a man she could share her life with.

Shocked by a sudden rush of longing, she dragged her gaze away.

'Are you okay?' he asked. 'Are you cold?' He put his arm around her as though to protect her from the bleak winter, and she relished that warm and comforting touch.

'I'm all right,' she said. She tried to gather her thoughts and send them somewhere where it was safe to venture. 'I expect you have your hands full these days, with work in A and E, the rescue services and looking after Kyle. I don't suppose you've had time to do any work on the barn conversion?'

He kept his arm around her, and she tried to tell herself that she shouldn't read anything into that. He was just being thoughtful and making sure that she was all right.

'It's still going along well enough. The oak floors have been laid, and the walls have been painted in very pale colours, so all that remains now is to choose the décor. Maybe you'd like to come over tomorrow afternoon and help me do that? I can't really do it this evening because Kyle goes to bed early, but tomorrow he'll be able to bring his toys along with him and he can play while we talk.'

'Sounds good to me.'

'Then we're on. It's a date…sort of.' He laughed, looking into her eyes, his mouth curving in amusement.

'Are we going to get the tree?' Kyle appeared

by his side and tapped him on the knee to drag his attention away from Jasmine.

Ben took a moment to pull his thoughts back on track. 'Oh, you've finished playing, have you?'

Kyle nodded.

'We'd better make a move, then.' Ben let his arm slide from Jasmine's shoulders, and instantly her feeling of well-being disappeared. He got to his feet. 'Straight along the path,' he told him. 'No wandering off. We don't want to lose you and have to send the dogs out, do we?'

'Big dogs, like huskies?' Kyle appeared to find that notion interesting.

'Bigger, probably. There's a lot of forest to search if anyone goes missing. So you'd better stay close.'

They inspected all the trees along the way, but Kyle wasn't satisfied with any of them.

'Too small,' he said, or, 'The shape's all wrong,' or, 'Some of the branches are wonky.'

They came across a small stream, its crystal-clear waters bubbling over rocks, with ancient trees lining its route. Kyle stepped into it gingerly, testing his footing, and then laughed gleefully as the water splashed around his feet. 'It's washed all the snow off my boots,' he said.

'So it has.' Ben let him play for a little while longer and then flicked a glance towards the fir trees. 'We'd better sort something out soon,' he said, 'or your mother will be coming home to an empty corner where she expects a beautiful display.'

'You know, Kyle, there are some beautiful Scots pines over there, just along that other path,' Jasmine said. 'They're a lovely blue-green colour, and the needles are usually soft, so they won't prickle when you put the baubles in place. And they smell lovely, too. How about looking at one of those?'

'Okay.' Kyle was happy to oblige and they turned off in that direction, following a winding path.

'I like this one,' he said, when they came upon the cluster of trees. He had picked out the tallest one around. He went up to it, standing close to the lower branches. Then he looked up and giggled as the pine needles tickled his face. 'I can't see the top,' he said. 'It's gone right up into the sky.'

'That's the one, is it? It looks magnificent,' Ben told him. 'I think you made a good choice there.' He gave a satisfied nod. 'It smells wonderful, too, just as Jassie said. I'll tell the forestry man that's the one we want.'

He was about to step back onto the path when a snowball hit him squarely in the neck and stopped him in the tracks. 'Who...? What...?' Ben looked around for the culprit, and then his gaze settled on Kyle, who was giggling fit to burst the zip on his coat. Another snowball splattered on Ben's shoulder, and then another one flew in quick succession to disintegrate on Jasmine's jacket.

'Right,' they said in chorus. 'Where is he? Let's get him.'

Kyle darted behind the tree as Ben and Jasmine scrambled to gather up snow, and after that it was a free-for-all, with snowballs flying in all directions. They were all laughing, squealing and shaking themselves down as the snow melted and left icy runnels here and there.

Jasmine cleared ice water from her face and neck and spluttered, gasping with the cold, while Ben chased Kyle and swooped on him, gathering him up into his arms. 'Enough, monster,' he said. 'Now we'll have to go to the café to warm up.'

Kyle nodded in excitement. 'Can I have a toasted sandwich? And some pop?'

'I think we can run to that.' Ben looked him in the eye. 'If I put you down, do you promise not to throw any more snowballs?'

Kyle looked as though that might be a trifle more difficult than he could manage.

'We're talking ham and cheese melt, here,' Ben reminded him. 'Think about it. Toasted sandwich, snowball…which one's going to win?'

'Ham and cheese,' Kyle conceded, and Ben carefully lowered him to the ground.

'Okay. I'll order the food and settle you and

Jassie at a table and then I'll go and arrange for someone to cut the tree.'

The café was a cheerful place, bright and warm, with clean pine tables and chairs and greenery all around to add a natural touch to the surroundings. Jasmine and Kyle chose a table by the window where they could look out at the paved terrace with its wooden benches and seats and, beyond that, the beginnings of the forest.

Jasmine ordered soup, and it arrived just as Ben returned from talking to the woodcutter.

'Mmm…that smells good,' he said, sniffing appreciatively. 'They make it themselves, you know, in the kitchens, from fresh ingredients that they grow on the land here…carrots, turnips, leeks, potatoes. It's the kind of thing I had in mind for the stable block—a chance to sell off fresh produce. Maybe fruit from the orchard, for a start. There are some really old varieties of apple trees on the land, as well as plums and pears.'

Jasmine dipped her spoon into the steaming hot soup. 'That sounds the sort of thing that

Callum would like…though he'd want his mainstay to be the sale of plants. He had a vision of running an open garden, showing people various ways of landscaping and offering them the chance to buy whatever they need on site. It's an ambitious project, and I suppose it would take a fair bit of money for him to get started. I know he's been saving hard, and he's talking of getting a loan from the bank to start his own business.' She savoured the taste of the soup. 'Of course, the banks aren't so keen to lend these days.'

'That's true.'

He sat down as the waitress brought his meal, lasagne with chips on the side. 'I'm ready for this,' he said, tucking in. Kyle was eating his toasted sandwich, swinging his legs under the table and looking around at the display on the wall showing a map of the forest and its attractions.

'I've been amazed at how well you've done these last few years,' Jasmine said, giving Ben a quick glance. 'Considering that you had so much opposition from your father in the beginning.

You said that he held back your trust fund, so much of what you did, buying up property and so on, must have been done on your own merit.'

He swallowed a forkful of pasta. 'I suppose I succeeded *because* of my father. He used to manage my grandmother's investments and would have sold Mill House if I hadn't stepped in. She was beginning to be confused as she went into old age, but I managed to gain power of attorney over her interests and stopped him from selling up. From then on, I was on my own. He couldn't forgive me for interfering, but I knew I had to make things work, for her sake.'

'So it gave you a taste for developing property?'

'That's right. And it's good to have an interest outside medicine. It helps to give your mind something to work on when things don't go the way you want them to. We'd all like things to go smoothly every time, but life isn't like that.'

'I know what you mean.' She finished off her soup, and the waitress brought a meat pasty to the table. Jasmine accepted it with a smile. 'Thanks.'

She studied Ben's brooding features. 'Have you had any more luck with getting your father on your side?'

He shook his head. 'I went to see him again the other day, but his attitude was cool. I wanted to find out what arrangements he'd made for Christmas, and I was planning on inviting him over to Mill House for the day, but I didn't get the chance. It was as though by being there I was reminding him of things he didn't want to think about.'

She frowned. 'Like what?'

'It was just a feeling I had. At one point I was looking at the grandfather clock in the study and I said I remembered the casing used to stick sometimes. He just changed after that. Where he'd been guarded and stilted before, he became positively cool. I guessed he wanted me to leave.'

'Was there something special about the clock, something significant, perhaps?'

He frowned, deep in thought. 'Not that I recall. When I was very small, I used to open the glass door and put my toy soldiers inside, so that they could hide from the enemy. I was always being told that it would interfere with the workings of the clock, but as far as I know, it didn't stop me.'

Jasmine smiled. 'I expect it was difficult for your father, coping with a small boy after your mother died.'

He nodded. 'I suppose so.' He looked across the table at Kyle, who was off in a dream world of his own, his toasted sandwich held to his mouth as though someone had pressed the pause button on the video. 'Who knows what he had to contend with?'

He gave his attention back to his lasagne, and then added, 'He did tell me that your father had arranged an appointment for him at the surgery and he was planning on keeping it, so that's a positive result.'

'I'm glad.' Jasmine finished off her pasty and wiped her hands on a serviette. 'You know, perhaps the only way to win your father round is to keep batting at the door. Maybe you could take him a hamper from the Mill Bakery and I could add some mince pies and a bottle of my father's elderberry wine—or does he only like the sort you have in your cellar?'

'I'm sure he'd appreciate a bottle of elderberry. Something that a person has taken the time and trouble to make themselves has to be special, doesn't it?' He laid a hand on hers. 'That's a great idea, Jassie. Perhaps we could go over to the manor together—say tomorrow, before we go over to the barn?'

She nodded, but then a thought crossed her mind. 'Does he know about Kyle?'

He shook his head. 'No, but he will after to-morrow, won't he? He knows that Anna is in hospital, but I still have to break it to him that she'll be staying with me afterwards.'

'It's tough, isn't it, dealing with fractious relatives?' Her mouth made a downward turn. 'I've never really experienced it until now. My family's always been close knit, and whenever there's a problem, we rally round one another.'

His eyes narrowed slightly. 'You're thinking of Callum?'

She nodded.

'He'll come round, eventually. For as long as I've known you, I've envied the way your family hangs together. I think of how it will be at your house on Christmas Day, with your mother presiding over the Christmas dinner and your father carving the turkey. Your aunt and uncle and cousins will be there, and I expect you'll all be wearing paper hats from the Christmas crackers and reading out the corny jokes and falling about laughing. I envy you that, Jassie.'

He looked into her eyes. 'It's something I've never experienced, and somehow I think that being with you would make it all the more special.'

She felt his fingers curl around hers, and with that simple touch he, filled her heart with pure joy. He wanted to be with her. He had said it. What more could she ask?

And then she remembered that Anna would be spending Christmas with him, and Kyle would be opening his toys in front of the fire at Mill House on Christmas Day, and the brief joy that had seared her soul quickly turned to ashes.

CHAPTER EIGHT

'Is HE coming back soon?' Kyle was watching the kitchen door, willing it to open. He'd been doing that for the last half-hour, and Jasmine decided it was time to distract him. She started to gather together the ingredients for a baking session.

'I'm not sure how long Ben will be,' she told him. 'He had to go out with the mountain rescue team to find someone who has been hurt. I expect he'll call us as soon as he's on his way back.'

Kyle was clearly not happy with that answer. 'But we were going to the big house and he was going to show me the secret hiding place. Why can't he come back now?'

'Because helping people who are injured is his job. Just imagine that you had hurt your knee,

Kyle.' Jasmine finished setting out flour, sugar and spices on the kitchen table. 'If it was a really bad pain, you'd want somebody to help you and take the pain away, wouldn't you?'

He nodded solemnly.

'Well, the man on the mountainside banged his knee when he slipped and fell, and it's very swollen and hurts a lot, so Ben has gone to help make him better. As soon as the man is safely in hospital, Ben will come back here and we'll all go off to the manor house as we planned.'

She added butter to the assembled items and then let her glance sweep over the kitchen table. 'In the meantime,' she said, 'we've all the ingredients here that we need to make cookies—and I have all these lovely Christmas cookie cutters. Look, there's an angel…and a Christmas tree…'

'And a Christmas stocking…and a bell.' Kyle laughed gleefully. 'Can I cut some, Jassie… please? I'd like to do that.'

'Of course you can. And afterwards, when

they're cooked, we'll ice them and put little silver balls on some of them.'

'Yes-s-s!' Kyle's excitement was growing by the minute, but he stopped and stood very still as someone knocked on the kitchen door.

'Jassie?' The door opened a notch and Callum peered into the room. 'Is it all right if I come in?'

'Of course.' Callum was the last person she expected, and seeing him now made her more than a little uneasy. They hadn't spoken properly since the other day when he had been upset about her seeing Ben, and now she wondered if he was about to go on where they had left off. With Kyle listening in, that would make life difficult. 'Come in,' she said, 'but perhaps you could make yourself useful and put the kettle on. I'm parched and I've no time to stop. We're about to have a serious cookie-making session here.' She sent him a swift glance, trying to gauge his mood. Maybe he wanted to declare a truce.

Callum did as she suggested, and then came

to sit down at the table. He looked curiously at Kyle. The little boy was lifting up each one of the cookie cutters, examining them carefully in turn.

'This one's my favouritest,' Kyle said, holding up the star for him to see. 'This goes over the stable, see?' He laid them out on the table, placing the star over the stable, and putting the angel next to both. 'And then we can have a tree over there.' He looked at Jasmine. 'Have you got any green icing? And we need white for the angel, yellow for the stable and silver for the star.'

Callum smiled. 'I think we have a budding artist here. He knows exactly what he wants, doesn't he?'

Jasmine nodded. 'He does.' She was busy making dough, but at the same time she was anxious to know what had prompted Callum's visit. Perhaps he just wanted to talk about Anna.

'I heard you'd been over to the hospital to see Anna,' she said. 'It must have come as a shock to learn that she'd had such a difficult time of it.' She glanced at Kyle to see if he was taking any notice of what they were saying, but he was engrossed in rolling out the dough, concentrating hard, his tongue peeping out from between his lips.

'Yes, I've been to see her several times. I was stunned. I had no idea that she had a heart problem,' he answered softly. 'I don't understand why she didn't tell me when we were together.'

Jasmine shot him a quick glance. 'Perhaps she didn't know how. Sometimes these congenital defects are missed, especially if they don't give any problems early on. Trouble can set in later, though, and sometimes the defect can be repaired. In Anna's case they decided that wasn't possible, and a new valve was the best option. It should give her a much better quality of life.'

'Maybe.' Callum frowned. 'But you could have told me all this before. You knew. Why did it have to stay secret?'

Jasmine paused, laying down her rolling pin. 'I didn't know myself until recently, when Ben told me. He said Anna didn't want anyone to know.'

'I still don't get it.' The lines in Callum's brow furrowed deeper. 'For her condition to get this bad, it must have been coming on for some time, so she probably knew way back when she left Woodsley. Why would she not say anything? And then to go and get pregnant, knowing that she had a problem that could become worse as a result seems like madness to me.'

Jasmine was thoughtful for a moment or two. 'Unless, of course, she only found out about the illness when she became pregnant. That could account for a lot of things. She was often breathless and sometimes complained of dizziness, but as far as I know she never went to see a doctor about it. Perhaps everything changed when she became pregnant.'

Callum mulled that over for a while. 'That makes a kind of sense. I suppose you could be right.' A look of melancholy crossed over his face. 'All I know is that when she left just after New Year, I was devastated. I couldn't understand what was happening. I knew she had been seeing more and more of Ben, but I wasn't expecting her to leave with him. I don't think I ever really got over the shock.'

'I know.' She said the words softly, on a ragged sigh. 'I always thought you and she were made for each other, but perhaps the thought of you going away to university was too much for her. After all, you weren't eighteen, you were twenty-one, and she might have expected you to have bypassed that kind of extensive education.'

He winced. 'Well, you know how it was. I was never as clear thinking as you. I couldn't make up my mind what I wanted to do, so I tried working at all kinds of different jobs. Then I discovered horticulture and realised it was something I could do for the rest of my life, even go into business for myself, but I needed to get the best qualifications possible. I suppose that must have come as a shock to Anna.'

Jasmine nodded. 'It could be what pushed her into leaving. You and she had always been a couple, but she probably thought the relationship wouldn't stand the strain of you being away at university. And then I guess people started to talk. Village life can be very closed in, with everybody knowing everything about everyone else. It could have been too much for her. She always used to join in with village activities, and I thought she was content here, but perhaps she needed a bit of space. Maybe that's why she turned to Ben, and when he said he was leaving she realised she could go with him and put everything behind her.'

'Yes, that's possible, but I still think we could have made a go of it if he hadn't started cosying up to her.' He contemplated that for a moment or two, frowning, but then he seemed to brace himself. 'Anyway, I'm glad she came through the surgery all right. It must have been a scary prospect for her.' He pressed his lips together. 'When I went to see her this morning, she was talking about going to the village carol-singing event on the green next Friday, but I don't think that will be a good idea, do you? She said Ben had to go because he was supposed to be helping out with the refreshment stall. The vicar roped him in, she said.' He grinned. 'She said he thinks the vicar's making him do penance for all his youthful misdeeds.'

Jasmine chuckled. 'More than likely.' She handed Kyle a cutter and showed him how to press it down into the dough. 'But you're right, it's probably best if she keeps away from crowds for the time being. Now that she's had a new heart valve fitted, she'll have to guard against infections. It's probably even more important at this stage, when she's fresh from surgery.'

'Hmm. That's what I thought.' He was silent for a moment or two. 'Maybe I'll suggest to her that she comes over to Mum's house instead. I don't know what Ben had in mind, but I can't imagine she'll want to be alone at Mill House. I know Mum and Dad are planning on going out for the evening to take part in the festivities, but I doubt they'll mind her coming over. And I'm sure we can find a bed for Kyle in the spare room, so that he can sleep over.'

She glanced at him from under her lashes.

'That sounds like a good idea, if she'll agree. I doubt she'd be up to standing around for long, anyway.' Knowing Ben, he would have made plans to do his stint at the refreshment stall and then he would return home instead of staying to enjoy the events.

'Yes, she said she was still feeling a little groggy. The anaesthetic can stay in your system for quite a while, can't it? And, of course, she's still healing.'

'That's true.'

He looked at Kyle's efforts with the cookie shapes. 'You've done really well there, lad. They'll be great when they've been baked in the oven.'

Kyle gave him a beaming smile. 'You have to press them down really hard, like this…else they don't cut properly.' He demonstrated, using the flat of his hand to press down on the cutter. 'You can make some, if you like,' he added generously. His face became instantly stern. 'But you have to wash your hands or you're not allowed.'

'Oh, I see. I'd better do that, then, hadn't I? And maybe I should make the tea, as well.'

They were on their second pot of tea an hour later when Ben returned from his rescue mission. 'Callum,' he said, nodding towards him. 'It's good to see you again. Are you home for the holidays?'

'I'm off for Christmas and New Year,' Callum answered, his manner remote. 'I suppose it's possible you could be working over the holiday period, isn't it? I know Jass has managed to get both days off this year.'

Jasmine gave a wry smile. 'Only because I've worked every one for the last several years,' she said. 'I thought it was time I had the option of staying home, and Mum particularly wanted me to help out this year. We have relatives coming over and there's a lot of work to do.'

'I'm off on Christmas Day,' Ben murmured. He turned as Kyle tugged on his shirt. 'What is it, Kyle?'

'Come and see the cookies I made.' Kyle dragged him over to the side of the room where the cookies were spread out on the worktops on baking trays, iced and gleaming, making a colourful array.

'They look super-scrumptious, don't they?' Ben exclaimed. His mouth curved. 'Good enough to eat, I'd say.' His hand swooped over the trays as though making a selection, and Kyle stopped him, pulling on his shirtsleeve.

'We saved you some. Over here, see…an angel and a star. I made them.'

'They're just perfect, aren't they?' Ben bit a corner off the star and savoured the taste. 'Mmm…delicious. Best I've ever tasted.'

Kyle's eyes glowed with pleasure, and his whole body seemed to puff up with pride. 'I've saved some for Mummy as well…the very prettiest angel with silver on her wings, and a star with lots and lots of silver balls.'

'She'll love them,' Ben said. 'She'll think they're the best cookies she ever had.'

Kyle's face was one big smile. Then he said in an accommodating tone, 'Callum made some as well, but his icing went a bit wrong. We had to put silver balls to hide the bits where it went too thick, and some of the icing got a bit squashy where he pressed them in…but he did all right, really.'

Callum tried to keep a straight face. 'Cooking never was my strong point,' he said. 'Give me a plant and I can make it grow and thrive, but baking I leave to those who do it best…like Jass and your mum.'

Jasmine chuckled. 'Still, you're right about the plants. I envy you your green fingers.'

Kyle peered closely at Callum's hands. 'They're not green,' he said. 'Only a bit when he used the green icing.' He frowned. Grown-ups were clearly a little odd.

Callum smiled, and stood up. 'I have to go,' he said. He lightly ruffled Kyle's hair and added, 'Thanks for helping me with the cookies. You were great.' Then he gave Jasmine a quick hug. 'See you later, Jass.'

He nodded towards Ben, almost as an afterthought, a cool, superficial nod, as though he was only doing it because the rules of good manners demanded it of him. Then he closed the door behind him.

'He still hasn't changed his opinion of me, has he?' Ben commented. 'His feelings for Anna must be stronger than anyone could have imagined.'

'Yes, they are.'

Jasmine prepared a basket with cookies, mince pies and a bottle of elderberry wine. 'I take it your father is expecting us?' she murmured.

He nodded. 'I told him you and your mother wanted him to have some goodies for Christmas in return for all the sound financial advice he's given your father over the year. I think he would have liked to say don't bother, but I didn't give him the option. I said it was a done deal, and then I rang him to let him know that we'll be late.'

'Good.' She glanced at the bottle of wine. 'Will he be all right drinking this if he has hypertension? Perhaps I should exchange it for another gift?'

'I doubt he'll drink it all in one go,' Ben

remarked. 'I don't suppose a small amount will do him much harm.'

'Are we going, then?' Kyle asked, coming to stand between them. With the baking out of the way, his impatience was growing, and Jasmine could see trouble brewing if they didn't soon make a move.

'Right away,' Ben said.

'Best foot forward.' Kyle looked down at his feet and started with his left foot.

Jasmine gave a wry smile. 'You're going to have to put him right on that one,' she told Ben. 'He's a very astute little boy, and he takes in everything you tell him, like a sponge.'

Ben laughed. 'I will.'

They arrived at the manor house some half an hour later, but by then Kyle was a trifle subdued. The long, sweeping drive had left him in awe of the place to begin with, and now, standing in front of the glorious eighteenth-century house, with its Georgian façade, his eyes grew wide. 'Does your daddy live here all by himself?' he asked, sending a swift glance towards Ben, who nodded.

Kyle frowned but said nothing more, and Jasmine said softly, 'The house seems more beautiful every time I see it. Given its age, you wouldn't expect that, would you?'

'Perhaps not, but a good deal of love and care has gone into it over the years. Parts of it date back to the sixteenth and seventeenth centuries, but the majority of the building is eighteenth century.'

Stuart Radcliffe opened the door to them. He was a tall, distinguished-looking man, a smattering of silver threaded through his once dark hair. Now, though, he appeared uncomfortable, as though visitors were the last thing he wanted, but he put on an expression of welcome for Jasmine, and then looked down at the child.

'You must be Kyle,' he said. 'I've heard all about you from Dr Brett...Jasmine's father.' The look he gave Ben was a clear reproof, as if his son had made a glaring omission. 'Come in, all of you. We'll go into the drawing room.'

'Are we going to draw?' Kyle asked, picking up on the word. 'Do you have crayons and pencils? I like to draw pictures.'

'Um…no…not exactly…' Stuart looked perplexed. 'It's just a name…for when people used to withdraw to another room after dinner.'

Kyle was puzzled. 'We don't do that. We generally stay in the kitchen, or I go to play in my bedroom.'

'Yes, well…um…' Stuart's voice tailed off. He led the way along the hall and showed them into a large room dominated by a grand fireplace, finished with an ornate Chippendale mantelpiece.

The furnishings in here were sumptuous, with comfortable settees and chairs, and there were floor-to-ceiling windows giving views over the beautifully maintained gardens.

'Please, sit down.' He waved them to a sofa, and then glanced distractedly around. 'I hear the boy's mother's in hospital,' he said, glancing towards Kyle, who was giving the room a systematic survey.

'That's right,' Ben said. 'She'd been ill for some time, but Wellbeck Hospital seemed the best place for her to have the operation. The cardiology department here has always monitored her condition, and I think she wanted to come back to her roots for such a major operation. Wellbeck has a good track record for heart surgery.'

'So I've heard.' Stuart frowned, looking uncomfortable once more, and Jasmine thought now might be the appropriate time to offer her gift.

'My mother sent you mince pies, and the elderberry wine is from my father,' she told him. 'He was really pleased with the advice you gave him about putting the surgery onto a better financial footing. And the cookies are courtesy of Kyle and me. We had a baking session this morning. Very messy, a lot of flour and icing sugar all over the place, but we had a great time making them.'

'I… Thank you…' Stuart's reaction wasn't quite what she'd expected. He seemed a little taken aback, at a loss for words, and she couldn't fathom what was going through his head.

'Are you all right?' she asked. 'I can exchange the wine for something else, if you'd rather?'

'No…no…not at all.' He pulled in a steadying breath. 'It just struck me that I have such a large kitchen here, with all the modern, high-tech equipment installed, and it's hardly ever used.' His eyes were troubled. 'Not for something as exciting as cookie making, anyway.' He seemed sad all at once, and Jasmine felt a strong pull of emotion towards him. Ben's father was not what he seemed. She was sure there were layers beneath that surface that, as yet, no one had uncovered.

Ben went to offer him the hamper he had brought with him, but Kyle stalled him, asking Stuart what was uppermost in his mind.

'Don't you have any pencils at all?' He tugged on Stuart's trouser leg and his chin jutted as he tried to gain his attention. 'My mummy always finds things for me to do, so's I don't get bored.' He looked into Stuart's eyes. ''Cos it isn't very good if I'm bored, you know. I get up to things, Mummy says.'

Ben stifled a chuckle, and Stuart was startled into paying the boy some heed. 'Ah…' he said. 'Well, then…uh…perhaps I can find you a pencil or two, and some paper.' He stood up and looked about him distractedly. 'Yes, let me see.'

He went over to the bureau to one side of the room and rummaged through various drawers.

Coming back to Kyle a moment or two later, he said, 'Here we are. Will this do?' He handed the boy several sheets of white paper, along with a couple of graphite pencils. 'You can sit over there at the table.'

Kyle peered up at him. 'Thank you.' He gave him a sympathetic smile. 'You don't know much about children, do you?' he said, showing a wise head on young shoulders. 'But it's all right. My mummy says we have to be kind to old people who don't understand about us. Noise hurts their ears, she says, and they don't like lots of running about.' He pondered that for a second or two. 'Which is a shame 'cos I love running and jumping and making lots of noise.'

Ben put his hand over his mouth to hide a grin, while Jasmine tried not to laugh out loud and turned her response into a cough instead. Stuart, on the other hand, was more confounded than ever.

'I…uh… I don't know about that, Kyle. I only had the one son, Ben, and as I recall he didn't run about or make a lot of noise.'

'That's because you packed me off to my grandmother whenever you had the chance,' Ben said in a flat tone. 'And then when I was eight years old, you tried sending me off to boarding school.' He smiled wryly. 'Not that it worked. I made such a nuisance of myself that they sent me home.'

'And cost me a packet in school fees into the bargain,' Stuart responded, his mouth taut. 'How could I cope with a young boy with more energy than a dynamo? I had a very high-powered job in the finance industry. There was no time for babysitting.'

'No, there wasn't,' Ben said. 'I noticed.'

'Perhaps you should show your father the hamper you brought him?' Jasmine put in hastily. The two men were building up to a confrontation and that was the very opposite of what they had set out to do.

Ben obliged, backing down.

'Thank you,' Stuart said, looking at the basket that was brimful of produce from the Mill Bakery. There was a Christmas cake, beautifully iced, with frost-covered fir trees and small sugar figurines depicting children dressed up in winter clothes playing in the snow. Ben had added jars of preserves, made from the autumn crops of fruits, and there was a large, honey-glazed ham.

'I know you like the hams that we sell at the bakery,' Ben said. 'And I've added a couple of jars of home-made chutney to go with it.'

'Thank you. I appreciate this.' Stuart's manner was restrained, and Jasmine sighed inwardly, despairing of the two of them ever becoming fully reconciled.

Kyle stepped into the breach. 'I made you a picture,' he said, waving a piece of paper under Stuart's nose.

'Oh.' Stuart looked at the pencil drawing, as though undecided which way round it should go, until Ben leaned across and turned it the right way up. 'Oh, I see. Thank you.' He still looked faintly bewildered, unsure about the precise nature of the picture.

Kyle gave a disgruntled sigh. 'It's a big house, see, like this one, and there's a secret room inside it, where people could hide from the bad people that came to get them, or p'r'aps they put their treasure in there.' He jabbed a finger at the picture. 'That's a boy, hiding.'

Stuart's face cleared. 'Oh, I see it now. Ben's been telling you about the priest hole, has he?'

Ben nodded. 'He said he would show it to me.'

'Yes, we can do that. It's at the back of the

house, through the library.' Stuart glanced at Jasmine. 'You've never seen it, have you? I mean, you've been to the house on occasion over the years, but you haven't seen the secret passage or the hidden room?'

She shook her head. 'No, I haven't. I'd love to look at it, though.'

He led the way through the house to the library, a wonderful, oak-panelled room with a magnificent inglenook fireplace and bookshelves lined with leather-bound volumes. There were chairs upholstered in fine fabrics and a beautiful, burnished wood desk to one side.

Stuart paused by one of the bookcases and then waved Kyle over to him. 'Just bend down and reach your hand into the gap behind the bookcase,' he said. 'Now press your finger quite hard into the carved wooden flower pattern on the panelling.'

Kyle did as he was told, and a moment later there was a soft click and a section of the panelling moved inwards.

'Wow,' Kyle said, his eyes lighting up. 'That's cool!'

'There's only room for two at a time in there,' Stuart murmured. He looked at Ben. 'Perhaps you should go first and help him down the steps. Show him the secret passage, and then help Jasmine to find her way. I'll stay here and wait for you to come back. I don't seem to be able to manage stairs quite so well these days.'

'Because of your blood pressure?' Ben was immediately concerned.

'Yes. But Dr Brett is going to see me about that tomorrow. I spoke to him on the phone and he said something about diuretics to take away the excess fluid…and a diet plan to make sure I'm not overloaded with salt and so on.'

'Good.' He looked at his father. 'Perhaps you should sit and wait for us. We could be gone for a while if Kyle takes to exploring.'

'I'll do that. Take your time.'

Ben led the way down the stone-carved steps into the priest's hole, and Jasmine followed Kyle. It was eerie down there, with cold stone walls and a room barely big enough to move around in. There was another door at one end, again with a hidden catch, opening up into a secret passageway.

'Where does this come out?' Kyle asked. 'Is it another secret room?'

'You'll see,' Ben murmured. 'Just keep going until you come to the door at the end.'

'This one?' A few minutes later Kyle felt around the edges of the door, frowning as he looked for a way to open it. Then he ran his fingers along a small groove, and the door obligingly sprang open. He stepped out into a stonebuilt folly, with mullioned windows that let in the light of the afternoon sun.

Kyle's mouth dropped open. 'We're in a little house!' he exclaimed in delight. Going to a second door, he looked outside and said excitedly, 'We're in a garden…only there are walls all around.'

'That's because it's a sunken garden,' Ben explained. 'People may not know it's here because it's surrounded by hedges and shrubs that hide the wall from prying eyes, for the most part.'

'Wow! I love it!' Kyle went off to explore, his boots leaving footprints in the snow.

He disappeared behind a bank of shrubs, and Ben said quietly, 'He'll be all right. He won't be able to go far from here unless he finds the gate, and that's always locked.'

Jasmine looked around and smiled. 'What a great childhood it would have been, to explore that secret passage and this lovely little folly.' She glanced at him. 'It's a pity you didn't have brothers and sisters to keep you company.'

He gave a soft laugh. 'Just as well that I didn't. My father could barely cope with me.'

'True.' She gave a small shiver as the shock of cold air seeped into her bones, and he was instantly concerned.

'Are you cold? Come back inside the folly and I'll keep you warm.' He wrapped his arms around her, drawing her against him and gently rubbing warmth into her body with the gentle sweep of his hands. 'Thanks for coming with me today to see my father,' he murmured. 'I wasn't looking forward to making the visit on my own, but with you around he seems much more mellow.'

'I think he was a bit nonplussed by young Kyle,' she murmured, resting her cheek against his chest. She felt the steady beating of his heart and felt totally at peace with the world, as if this was where she was meant to be. His hand came to rest at the nape of her neck, lightly stroking the silk of her hair. 'It must be difficult for him,' she said. 'He's not used to children, and yet now he has to come to terms with the fact that he'll be around from now on. Kyle's part of your life, so he has to have a place in his.'

'I suppose he…' Ben broke off as Kyle came back into the folly.

'Why are you holding Jasmine?' Kyle asked, giving them a curious look.

'She was feeling cold.' Ben's glance wandered over him. 'You're covered in snow, so I guess you've had a good time out there.'

'Yes…I built a snowman. Come and see.'

Ben gave Jasmine one last squeeze, before reluctantly releasing her. 'Onward and upward,' he said. 'We'll have you back in the warm in a minute or two.'

'I'm fine now, thanks,' she said, but the truth was she wasn't fine at all. It had been a mistake to stay in his arms for even a few seconds, because it stirred up all kinds of yearnings inside her, and he could answer none of them. She loved Ben, but he had a unique bond with Anna and Kyle, and she didn't see where she fitted in. She was an outsider, looking in.

CHAPTER NINE

'Do you have the test results back on Mr Farnham?' Ben asked, coming to join Jasmine at the main desk in A and E.

'I do.' She handed him the lab report. 'There's a ninety per cent blockage of the blood vessel, so I've called the neurosurgeon for a consultation.'

'Good.' He gave a satisfied nod. 'I expect he'll want to operate straight away.'

He leaned back against the desk, idly scanning through various reports while Jasmine added her signature to the patients' charts she was working on. 'Thanks for helping me out with choosing the furnishings for the barn the other day. It didn't seem as though we had much time after we were late going to the manor house, but

I do appreciate your input. You've a real eye for textiles.'

'It was my pleasure. I thought what you'd done at the barn was wonderful. Very clean lines, so modern looking. It's wonderful.'

'Yes, I'm pleased with it myself. It's all coming along well.'

She went on signing charts. 'How is Anna coping now that she's out of hospital?' she asked after a minute or two. 'Has she settled in all right at Mill House?'

He looked up from the report he had been studying. 'I think she's doing okay…the best we can expect…though she's not really up to coping with a boisterous four-year-old just yet. I've arranged for Molly from the village to be with her during the day, to keep an eye on her and to look after Kyle while I'm at work. I would have left him with Carole, as before, but Anna wanted him to be at home with her. It's understandable, I suppose.'

'Yes.' Jasmine sent him a brief look from under her lashes. He cared a great deal for Anna, that was plain to see, and it went without saying that he thought the world of Kyle. She said softly, 'I heard that she wanted to go to the carol singing on the green tomorrow. Do you think she'll be up to it?'

He shook his head. 'I don't think it's a good idea, and we talked it through. It was mostly for Kyle's benefit that she wanted to do it. I told her I would take him there and keep an eye on him. Then I'll drop him back with her when I have to man the refreshment stall later on. She seemed happy enough with that compromise.'

He put the reports to one side. 'I left her looking over the plans for the interior of the barn conversion. She seemed to like the ideas you came up with…especially the textiles and the furniture. So all that's left to work on now is the kitchen. I gave her some brochures to sift through, and as soon as she decides on the units I can go ahead and order. One way or another it should all start to come together fairly soon. I'm hoping that it will all be finished not too long after Christmas.'

'Are you having Christmas at Mill House? I wondered if things might have improved enough with you and your father for him to invite you to the manor.'

His mouth turned down at the corners. 'That's not going to happen…though I have invited him to come and spend the holiday with us. He hasn't given me an answer yet.'

'I'm sorry.' Her gaze was sympathetic. 'Maybe he'll come round, given a little more time.'

'As though five years wasn't enough?' He gave a short laugh. 'To be honest, I've given up on the idea of spending Christmas together like a complete family. It isn't going to happen.'

'No, maybe not.' She laid a hand on his arm in a gesture of sympathy, and he responded by gently squeezing her hand. That simple action was enough to stir up all kinds of emotions in her. His warmth enveloped her, made her long for what she couldn't have, and above all she was saddened. She would be with her own family at Christmas, something she always cherished, and yet she would have given anything to have

Ben with her on that day. She was wishing for the impossible, of course. His priorities were marked out. He would be with Anna and Kyle, and somehow that seemed to be the only proper option.

'We have a patient coming in by ambulance,' the triage nurse said, hurrying over to them and shattering Jasmine's thoughts. 'He should be here in about ten minutes. It's a young boy, Mitchell, about three years old, wandered off and fell into an icy pond close to his home. His father pulled him out of the water, but he didn't appear to be breathing.'

Ben sucked in his breath. 'Are there any life signs?'

'Yes, but his pulse is barely discernible.' She looked anxious. 'His body temperature is twenty degrees C. He appeared lifeless, but the paramedics have started him on oxygen therapy and rewarming.'

'Good.' Ben was tense. 'Let's get everything set up to receive him. We'll need to check arterial blood gases, do a series of chest X-rays over the next few hours and set up a twelve-lead electrocardiogram.' He frowned. 'Jassie, I want you to set up an intravenous line and initiate cardio-respiratory monitoring. I'll intubate him and get him ready for extracorporeal membrane oxygenation and warming.'

Jasmine hurried away to prepare for the little boy's arrival. This was the kind of event every medical professional dreaded. There was no guarantee that they could pull him through. They might simply be too late.

Even so, the staff would work as a team to do whatever was possible to save him. They would circulate the child's blood through an oxygenating system that would gradually raise his temperature and ensure that adequate oxygen went to all the tissues of his body.

It was a desperately worrying situation, and when the child was brought in just a few minutes later, Jasmine was overwhelmed by compassion for him. He was just a baby, really. He was deathly pale, unresponsive and his life signs barely registered on the monitors. Her heart went out to his parents, who were white faced and distraught with grief.

Once they had put all the lifesaving measures in process, Ben began to explain the procedure to them, taking time to ensure that they knew what to expect. 'It will take some time for his temperature to come up to anything near normal,' he said. 'It could take several hours.'

'And will he be all right then? Will he recover?' It was a desperate plea.

'We're doing everything we can for him. Our aim is to get him to breathe on his own, but with near-drowning the outcome is not always straightforward. There could be complications, which we have to deal with as they occur.'

Jasmine knew he was trying not to give them false hope, yet he wanted to reassure them at the same time. For her part, she made the boy her prime focus for the rest of her shift, monitoring his condition continuously, praying for even some slight improvement.

Ben came to find her later that day. 'You're

still here? Shouldn't you have gone home a couple of hours ago?'

She looked at him wearily. 'I was hoping there would be some change in him. He's so pale, so still. It's heart-breaking, seeing him this way.'

He laid an arm around her shoulders. 'I know. I keep imagining how I would feel if it was Kyle lying there. It makes me shudder to think of it.' He let his gaze run over her. 'But you really should go home, you know. You've been on your feet for hours and you look washed out. There's nothing more you can do for him. Everything's in hand, and the nurses will let us know as soon as there's any change.'

She shook her head. 'I can't go home. I know they say we shouldn't get too involved with our patients, but this little boy wrings my heart to shreds. I'm going to stay here until I see that he's on the mend.'

Gently, he ran the backs of his fingers across her cheek and tucked back a lock of silky, chestnut hair that had escaped from its silver clip. 'I always knew you would make a good doctor,' he said softly. 'It makes me glad I came back here, knowing that you're around. You care about people, and you never give up on anyone, do you? I've seen how you are with other patients. But it isn't just here, at work, where it shows. You care about everyone.' He gave a wry smile. 'You stood by me all those years ago when people were ready to condemn me, even your own brother. I don't think I showed it at the time, but I appreciated how you went out on a limb for me.'

She gave a weary smile. 'I don't recall anyone listening. I wanted them to know that there are two sides to every story…that you had a messed-up childhood that was bound to turn you into a rebel. And as for Anna, who are we to judge what goes on in other people's relationships?' She didn't tell him that she'd grieved when he'd left and, besides, he would have found the notion incredible. After all, she had always kept her distance from him, hadn't she? It would have been all too easy to be sucked into his charismatic whirlpool.

'But people do.' His fingers were threading lightly through her hair, a caress soft as a whisper, and she doubted he was even aware of what he was doing. His touch sent delicate ripples of pleasure to eddy along her nerve endings, and heat surged in her cheeks. 'I thought by coming back here, I could begin to put things right, but I'm not sure that I'm succeeding very well. My father is as obstinate as ever, and the business people in the village are holding meetings to protest about the barn and stable conversion. They're a bit late, that's all I can say.'

She glanced up at him. 'They're just worried that whatever you have planned will put them out of business. You can hardly blame them for that.'

'True…but I don't have a strict plan of action as yet, and whatever I do will have to go before the planning committee. I don't see why they're concerned but, then, it's probably a hangover from the old days. Whatever Radcliffe does is bound to be bad news.'

'Are they likely to make you think twice about

staying? I mean, what will you do when your two months here come to an end?'

He frowned. 'I'm not sure yet. I've been offered a post back in Cheshire, so that's something I'll have to consider.'

Jasmine felt her throat close up. Of course, Anna would be happy to go back there, wouldn't she? Kyle had his roots there, and Anna had built up a business. Why had she even imagined that Ben might want to stay here in his home village? He had never been one for settling down.

She straightened, moving away from that absently caressing hand. It stopped her from thinking straight, and she had to hang on to her common sense right now. Falling for Ben had been a bad move. There was no future in it, and she should have stuck to her original plan... avoid him like the plague.

'A job offer has to be good news, doesn't it? At least it means you have one option already in the bag.' She looked at the little boy lying motionless on the bed. 'I think I'll go and take a break in the staff lounge for a while. You're right. I've been on my feet for too long.'

'I'll let you know if anything happens.'

'Thanks.'

She stayed in the lounge for some time, sitting in one of the armchairs and sipping coffee. The hot liquid was reviving, and it helped to clear her head. She would concentrate solely on her patients from now on and avoid getting any further entangled with Ben. Just being around him was disturbing to her peace of mind.

The nurse called her back to the treatment room just half an hour later. 'Mitchell's showing signs of pulmonary oedema,' she said, her tone urgent.

Jasmine was instantly on her feet. 'I'll come right away.'

She checked the child's X-rays and oxygen saturation level. 'His lungs are filling with fluid,' she told the nurse. 'We'll start him on diuretics right away. Let Ben know what's happening, will you?'

'I will. He had to go and deal with another

emergency, but I'll get a message to him right away.' She looked at the boy. 'Poor little chap. I wouldn't like to be the parent going through this agony. It's bad enough dealing with it from our side of the bed.'

'That's true.' Jasmine went back to the staff-room and as the night wore on she curled up on the sofa in there. She must have slept for a while, but when she woke in the early hours of the morning, she discovered that someone had thoughtfully laid a blanket over her. From the other side of the room there was a satisfying aroma of freshly made coffee, and as she struggled to sit up she saw that Ben was coming towards her, a steaming mug in each hand.

'I saw that you were beginning to stir,' he said, 'so I thought you might like this.' He handed her a mug and then sat down beside her on the sofa.

'Is there any news?' Jasmine couldn't hide her anxiety.

'His temperature's almost back to normal. We'll take him off the extracorporeal membrane oxygenation in a while and continue with normal warming measures.'

'And the fluid in his lungs?'

'We're still working on that. It'll take a while to clear. I shan't be happy until I see some signs that he's able to cope on his own.'

'No, of course not. How are his parents managing?'

'Reasonably well, I think, given what they're going through. He's warmer, but there's still no colour in his face.'

She sent him a quick glance as she sipped her coffee. 'Shouldn't you have gone off duty hours ago?'

He gave a sheepish grin. 'Like you, I couldn't go home knowing that a child was in such a dire condition.'

'Will Anna cope on her own?'

He nodded. 'I rang to check. Molly saw Kyle off to bed and then stayed for a while until he dropped off to sleep. Anna was watching TV earlier, but I'm sure she'll be tucked up in bed by now.'

They drank their coffee slowly, neither of them wanting to move just then. The hospital was quiet in these early hours. Even the flow of emergency admissions had slowed up. It was strange sitting here in the half-light, with Ben by her side. She felt the brush of his thigh against hers and struggled as the heat of that contact sizzled through her entire body. She swallowed more coffee. She would not let it faze her.

'Shall we go and check on Mitchell?' Ben suggested a few minutes later. 'Let's hope there's some good news.'

'Yes.' She rinsed the mugs at the sink and then followed him out of the door.

With Mitchell's body temperature back to normal, Ben set about removing the ECMO. Jasmine checked the monitors to make sure that all was as it should be, and then she gazed down at the small child.

'Is he going to be all right?' his mother asked, her eyes reddened with the strain of keeping watch over him.

'We can't be sure how things will turn out at

this stage,' Jasmine said, 'but the monitors aren't showing anything that we didn't expect. We just have to make sure that his lungs are cleared of fluid, and we're waiting for some kind of response from him. Why don't you try holding his hand and talking to him for a while? You might manage to get a reaction.'

The woman did as she'd suggested, and Jasmine turned away to write up Mitchell's charts. Ben adjusted the dose of diuretic, and for the next hour everything was quiet in the room, except for the boy's mother's soft voice, telling him about the Christmas presents waiting for him back home and how his sister was waiting for him to play with her on the karaoke machine.

The child coughed and seemed to stir, and in an instant Ben was at his bedside. 'I'm going to remove the tube from his throat,' he said, after a while, 'and we'll see how he manages on his own.'

'Will there be any damage to his brain?' his father asked worriedly, anxiety rapidly overcoming relief. He turned to Jasmine. 'I mean, he was under the water for several minutes. Is he going to remember who we are…or even be able to live a normal life after what's happened to him?'

'Hopefully, he'll be fine. Very cold water causes a reflex that protects the brain and organs from a lack of oxygen, so we'll hope for the best.'

With the tube removed from his throat, Mitchell coughed again and began to whimper, making soft mumbling sounds that Jasmine couldn't interpret.

'He's saying it's his turn on the karaoke,' his mother said, a broken sob in her voice but her mouth creasing into a smile. 'He and his sister are always arguing about it.' She stroked her son's hand and wept silently, the torment of the last fifteen hours breaking like a dam with her child's recovery.

Jasmine's gaze tangled with Ben's. The relief was overwhelming, and what she wanted most of all right then was to hug him and celebrate.

Perhaps he had the same idea because he nodded towards the door, and they left the parents alone with their son for a while.

Out in the corridor, he wrapped his arms around her and kissed her tenderly on the forehead. 'That was a good result,' he said, his voice rough around the edges. 'I'm glad we were both here to see it.'

'It was the best,' she murmured, loving the way he held her close in his embrace. 'The very best.'

Slowly, carefully, he released her with a sigh and drew back. 'I wish we were somewhere else,' he said, 'somewhere where I could hold you without fear of someone coming along.'

His comment brought her to her senses with a small jolt. 'There's the rub,' she whispered. 'There's always someone waiting in the wings. Life just doesn't turn out the way we want it to, does it?'

He looked at her oddly, but if he understood what she was saying, he didn't respond. 'You should go home and get some rest while you can,' he said. 'You still have another shift to do tomorrow, and then there will be the Christmas festivities waiting for you.'

'And for you. Maybe you should take your own advice.'

They went back into the treatment room to check on Mitchell once more. He appeared to be sleeping peacefully, and the monitors showed nothing untoward. 'We'll keep him on the diuretics for a while,' Ben told the boy's parents, 'and we'll continue with oxygen by mask, but everything seems to be going along reasonably well, so I'm hopeful that he's out of the woods now. I'm going to hand over to my colleague, and I'll see you both again tomorrow.'

Jasmine said her own goodbyes, and then headed out to the car park. As he had said, she had a full day ahead of her tomorrow—or rather today. And the carol singing was something she never missed. It wouldn't do for her to be look-ing peaky. Her parents would be there, along with her friends and most of the people from the village. She'd even heard that her father had encouraged Stuart Radcliffe to come along. Her father and Stuart seemed to have built up some kind of rapport, because apparently Ben's father had accepted an invitation to come to the house for drinks on Christmas Day afternoon.

The hours flew by once she managed to get some sleep. Refreshed, she went back to the hospital to start her shift and check on Mitchell once more. He was making a brilliant recovery, and after that she felt as though she was walking on air.

By the evening, she was wrapped up in warm clothes, a winter coat, scarf and hat, and leather boots to keep out the cold. Everyone gathered on the village green for the lighting-up ceremony, and on a signal from the vicar, the huge tree and all the surrounding streets became a blaze of colour. Then the carol singing began in earnest.

Ben held Kyle in his arms so that he could see what was going on, and the boy gazed around in wonder at the shimmering tree and the myriad stars that made up the street decorations. 'Mummy would like those,' Kyle said.

'She'll be able to see them soon,' Ben promised. 'When she's feeling a bit stronger.'

'That's what Callum said.' Kyle frowned. 'He took her to his house…his dad's house. I don't know why we couldn't stay at the mill.'

'I'm with you on that one, lad,' Ben murmured. 'But it was your mother's choice. She thought it would be a good thing to do.'

Kyle hunched his shoulders and looked around once more, taking in the sights and sounds all around him—the funfair that had been set up in the village square, the candyfloss stalls and the mobile unit selling beef burgers and bacon butties. He sniffed the air appreciatively.

Jasmine looked at Ben. 'Are you not comfortable with the fact that she's staying at my parents' house this evening?'

'I think it was a mistake to move her. It was disruptive and unnecessary when both she and Kyle were settled at my house.'

'But Callum wanted to keep her company,

and perhaps he wouldn't have felt right doing that at the mill. And as you say, it was Anna's choice. She had the option to stay but she chose to go with Callum. Is that what bothers you... that she's with my brother? Are you jealous?'

'Do I have anything to be jealous of?' He raised a dark brow.

'I'm not sure. Callum has never stopped loving Anna, and since she's come back to Woodsley he's been trying to see her whenever possible. If you don't like that, perhaps you are jealous.'

'Or it could be that I don't want her to be hurt. She's vulnerable. She's been through a lot these last few years.'

The carol singing came to an end a few minutes later, and the crowd dispersed. People cheerfully made their way towards the funfair or the bric-a-brac stalls. The atmosphere was good humoured, full of laughter and the joy of the Christmas season.

'What do you want to do first?' Ben asked Kyle, carefully lowering him to the ground. 'The funfair or the stalls?'

'The rides.' The answer was emphatic, and Kyle tugged eagerly at Ben's hand, impatient to get under way. 'I want to go on the horses that go up and down.'

'Okay, that's what we'll do, then.' He glanced at Jasmine. 'Luckily, Molly offered to look after the refreshment stall for the first half of the evening, so we should have plenty of time to fit everything in.'

'I could always watch him for you when you have to go and take over,' she volunteered, but he shook his head. 'It'll be his bedtime by then, anyway, but thanks for that.'

She went with them to the carousel and stood to one side, watching as the boy tried out as many of the rides as possible. Ben chatted with the vicar while keeping an eye on Kyle, and after a while she realised that Stuart Radcliffe had also come along to watch.

She sent him a quick smile. 'I wasn't expecting to see you here tonight,' she said. 'It's good that you were able to come along.'

'Your father persuaded me that it was the

right thing to do,' Stuart answered, with the air of a man who felt somehow out of place. 'He said the fresh air would do me good, and it was time I mixed in a bit more with village life.' His expression was rueful. 'He seems to think I'm in danger of becoming a recluse, and that will never do.'

Jasmine chuckled. 'My father was always one for straight talking…but I'm glad you took his advice.' She glanced at Kyle, who was holding on to the steering-wheel of a racing car, making brumming sounds as though he was on a real racetrack. 'It must be great for you to see your grandson enjoying himself.'

He didn't answer, and she added softly, 'I know all this must have come as a great shock to you, but at least Ben has done the right thing and brought him back here.'

He pulled in a shuddery breath. 'I'm not convinced that any of my son's actions are quite what they seem to the outside world.' He turned to her. 'He never introduced Kyle to me as my grandson, and even though everyone around here thinks that's so, I'm not sure of it. Kyle is a delightful child, and much as I would love to know that the boy is my own flesh and blood, I'm afraid I don't think that's possible. I don't believe that Ben is the boy's father.'

It was Jasmine's turn to suck in a shocked breath. 'You don't?'

He shook his head. 'Over the years, Ben and I have had our differences of opinion—sometimes quite forceful differences, as you probably know. I always thought he was a rebel, a stubborn, obstinate and wilful boy who grew into a stubborn, obstinate and wilful man.' He frowned. 'But over the last few months I've begun to realise that one thing above all marks him out among men. He's strong willed and determined, and he always goes straight for what he believes to be right, no matter whether anyone thinks otherwise. I just don't believe he's the kind of person who would get a girl pregnant and not insist on marrying her. I would stake my life on it. He has too much honour to consider any other course of action.'

Jasmine's mind was in a whirl. Could Stuart be right in what he was saying? She was struggling to take it all in, and it felt very much as though all the breath had left her body.

She took a moment or two to get herself together, then she said in a quiet voice, 'It sounds as though you have a lot of respect for your son.'

He nodded. 'I think I do. It's as though I've been blind for all these years, locked in my own preconceived ideas and beliefs, and now I'm beginning to see how things really are.'

She lightly touched his arm. 'Perhaps you should tell him how you feel?'

He didn't answer, and she guessed he was turning things over in his mind. She went back to watching the child on the carousel. Was Stuart right? Was it possible Kyle wasn't Ben's son after all?

CHAPTER TEN

'THAT was a delicious Christmas dinner, Mum.' Jasmine leaned back in her chair, full to the brim with turkey and stuffed bacon rolls, roast potatoes and all the trimmings. 'Everything was perfect.'

'Thank you. I'm glad you enjoyed it.' Her mother smiled. 'I hope you've saved some room for Christmas pudding.'

Jasmine ran a hand over her stomach. 'Maybe in a while, when this lot's gone down.'

Callum added his appreciation, and their uncle, aunt and cousins echoed what he'd said. Her father sat and surveyed the table, a contented smile on his face. There were sparkly table decorations as a centrepiece, gold-sprayed pine cones and red and gold poinsettia providing a glorious splash of colour. And throughout there were the remnants of Christmas crackers, their motifs chuckled over and discarded, and small trinkets abandoned along with an assortment of paper hats.

They all helped clear the table, and Jasmine began to load the dishwasher. It had been a wonderful Christmas Day so far, with the church bells waking her in the morning, and when she had drawn back the curtains it had been to look out onto gently falling snow. Soft flakes had drifted on the air and begun to slowly cover everything in their path with a coat of white.

Only one thing was missing. The day would have been perfect if Ben was there. But, of course, he was at Mill House, with Anna and Kyle, and there was probably no chance that she would be able to see him at all today. Going to visit him would seem like an intrusion, and yet it was what she wanted most of all.

They sat down at the table once more for Christmas pudding, brought to the table in a haze of pale blue flame and served with brandy cream. Jasmine ate a small portion and thought about all the patients in hospital who would be eating their own Christmas dinners, hopefully in the company of family and friends who had come to visit.

Mitchell was still recovering and was well enough to sit up now. He had been chatting to his parents when she'd checked that morning. Santa had done a round of the wards, giving gifts to all the children unfortunate enough to be in hospital, and the adults had been rewarded with impromptu entertainment and a string of hilarious jokes from the senior house officer on duty.

A couple of hours later, Jasmine and her family said goodbye to the relatives who had come to visit, and the house settled down to a comparatively quiet time. The TV was on, the Queen's traditional speech had been broadcast to all and sundry and there were films showing on most channels. Her father was dozing in his armchair by the fire.

Then the doorbell rang, and Jasmine guessed it was Stuart Radcliffe coming to join them for drinks as her father had suggested. She laid a hand on her father's shoulder and gently shook him awake. 'I think this must be Stuart come to visit,' she said. 'Are you ready to go and say hello to him?'

'Ah, yes. I'll be glad if he could make it. He's come out of his shell a lot over these last few weeks. Let's go and make him welcome.'

Only it wasn't just Stuart who was waiting at the door. Anna and Kyle were with him, and, to Jasmine's great joy, Ben was there, too.

'I'm so glad you came over,' she told him, giving him a hug. He looked fantastic, wearing dark chinos and a dark blue shirt beneath a winter overcoat that was open to flap loosely around his legs. 'I was wondering how your Christmas was going.'

'It's been really good so far,' he said with a smile. 'My father decided to accept my invitation, so that was great. It feels like a new beginning somehow.'

'That's wonderful.' She showed him into the

living room, and her father added his greetings, inviting them to sit down.

'I'm glad you could all drop by,' he said. 'I did suggest that Stuart bring you along with him, but I wasn't sure whether you would want to do that, especially if you were full up with all the Christmas food—not to mention that Kyle must be eager to play with the toys Santa brought him.'

He looked at Kyle. 'I see you've brought a couple of toys with you. Did Santa bring you some nice things?'

Kyle nodded vigorously. 'I had a red fire engine and a racing track so the cars go round and round.' He demonstrated with his hands, making whirring noises as though he was on the circuit. 'And there was a robot that walks and talks, and a remote control car. And lots of things.' He waved his fire engine under everyone's noses and followed up with a box kite that was decorated like a bird in flight. 'Ben gave me the fire engine and Callum bought me the kite. Mummy says we might go and fly it later on today if we have time.'

'Well, it's stopped snowing, and there's a bit of a wind starting up, so you might be all right to do that. I dare say the snow will keep the darkness at bay for a while.' Callum was smiling as he looked at the boy. 'I'm glad you're pleased with all your presents.' He sat down with Anna and the boy on the settee, inspecting the kite to see how many brightly coloured trailers it had, while Jasmine's father went to fetch drinks for everyone.

Stuart was talking to their mother, and Jasmine excused herself to go and get ice from the freezer.

'Do you need any help?' Ben asked, following her into the kitchen.

'Thanks,' she said. 'Perhaps you could tip the cubes into the ice bucket for me. I always have trouble getting them out.'

He obliged, giving the tray a sharp tap with his hand, and the ice cascaded into the container.

She gave him a rueful look. 'Whenever I do that, they scatter all over the place.'

They went back into the living room. Kyle was still talking to Callum about the kite. 'You have to go up a hill and let it catch the wind,' he said, 'and if it's a good kite, it will go way up in the air, like this.' He stretched his hand out to the ceiling.

'It sounds as though you've flown a kite before,' Callum said, and Kyle nodded.

'I had one for my birthday, but it got tangled up in a tree and it broke. I cried, 'cos I really liked that kite.'

Callum gave him a thoughtful glance. 'When is your birthday, Kyle? Do you know?'

'June. I don't know the date, but Mummy said the sun was shining and it was really hot.'

Callum looked at Anna. 'So he's actually four and a half years old?'

'Yes.' It came out as a whisper, and as soon as she had said it, she stood up and went over to the window, looking out over the snow-laden garden.

Jasmine gazed at her brother. He must surely be putting two and two together and coming up with the fact that Anna had been pregnant before she'd left Woodsley Bridge. Was it possible that Kyle was Callum's son?

She glanced at Ben, who was helping to hand out drinks. His gaze meshed with hers, a faint smile curving his lips. 'Seems like now would be a good time for flying a kite,' he murmured, handing a glass to Callum. 'Anna's much stronger now, and I expect she would be able to manage the short walk to Brier's Field, if you take things slowly. It isn't hilly, but the wind blows across the meadow and Kyle would have a great time, I'm sure.'

'Good idea,' Callum said. He was staring at Anna. 'Maybe we could go as soon as we finish our drinks?'

Anna nodded cautiously. She looked towards Jasmine's parents. 'I feel perhaps it would be rude to leave so soon, when you've been kind enough to invite us over.'

'Heavens, girl, you don't need to worry about

that,' Jasmine's mother said. 'You young things need to get out, and it's a shame not to catch what's left of the light. You go off and enjoy yourselves.'

Her father echoed that. 'Sounds as though you two have a good deal to talk about, anyway,' he said, in his usual straightforward manner, and Jasmine inwardly groaned. Tact wasn't his strong point.

Ben leaned towards her. 'Maybe you and I could take a walk over to the mill in a while?' he suggested in an undertone. 'It appears to me that Anna and Callum aren't the only people who have things they need to clear up between them.'

'I think you're right,' she said softly. 'Even your father guessed that everything wasn't as it seemed.'

He gave her a crooked smile. 'It just goes to show there are times when he can be surprisingly astute.'

They gave it a decent interval before they left, chatting with Stuart and Jasmine's parents for a while. 'We're going to take a walk over to Mill House,' Ben said at last. 'Perhaps we'll see you all later?'

'Of course.' Her mother saw them to the door. 'Don't worry about Stuart, he seems content to be with us.' She pulled in a quick breath. 'My word, this is turning out to be a day of happenings and new beginnings. Not at all what I expected, but absolutely wonderful.' She gave them both a beaming smile, and Jasmine wondered how much her mother knew of what went on in her heart…a lot more than she said, obviously.

It was a short walk to the mill. Jasmine's boots crunched in the snow, and she looked around her, marvelling at the sheer white light that was reflected from the ground. There were icicles hanging from the branches of the trees, cobwebs frozen and outlined in the hedgerows and the crystalline sparkle of snow overall. It was beautiful.

'I love it here,' she said, as they approached Ben's house. A cheerful light welcomed them in the porch, and there was a lovely old-world look about the place. It was perfect, with a thick blanket of snow on the roof and latticed windows like jewels in the fading light. 'I don't know how you could even think of leaving. And as to the house, you've put so much effort into it, and yet you've hardly lived here. Surely you'll miss it?'

He opened the front door and ushered her inside. 'A lot of what I decide to do will depend pretty much on what you have to say,' he murmured. He helped her off with her coat and then led the way into the sitting room.

As in his other properties, there were exposed beams about the place, polished wood floors, and in the sitting room a grand, open fireplace, where logs crackled and spat, sending a golden glow into the room. 'Sit down, and I'll get you a drink,' he said, indicating a luxuriously upholstered sofa. 'Would you like something alcoholic, or coffee, maybe?'

'Coffee, I think. I've had a tad too much alcohol already today. Any more and I might not be in control of my actions.'

'Well, there's something I'd like to see,' he said with a laugh. 'Perhaps I should make you a liqueur coffee?'

She sighed. 'Ah, now you've found my weak spot. I'm more than tempted. I can't resist.' She stood up. 'I'll come and help you make them.'

The kitchen was similarly old-worldly, a delightful combination of oak units, exposed beams and an island bar where they could sit and drink their coffee and look out over the back garden. Darkness was falling now, and Ben drew the curtains, so it felt as though they were cocooned in this tranquil oasis of calm.

'I think Callum will have realised by now that Kyle is his son, don't you?' Ben asked, coming to stand beside her as she was perched on the barstool.

'I imagine so…unless you and Anna were deeply involved some three months before you left the village?'

He gazed at her. 'You must know that isn't true. Anna and I have never been involved in that way. She was ill, she was vulnerable and she didn't know what to do for the best, so she turned to me. I told her to tell Callum that she was pregnant, but she wouldn't. She said he was going away and, anyway, what would he want with a girl who had a defective heart? It would put a blight on his life, she said.'

He pressed his lips together. 'Of course, I told her she was wrong and that he would stand by her, but she wouldn't hear of it. She thought he would stay with her out of pity and duty, and she didn't want that. So she decided to leave, and I've been keeping an eye on her ever since. She made me promise that I wouldn't say anything to anyone, because she didn't want Callum to find out.'

Jasmine sipped her coffee. 'I suppose I should have known when you didn't give me a straight answer, but you seemed so fond of Anna and Kyle, and I was sure there was more going on between you. She was even living with you from time to time, and then you brought her here, to the mill. That confused me.'

He slid his arms around her. 'What should I

have done? I could hardly leave her to fend for herself. She needed support through the operation and afterwards, and I was determined to give her that. Afterwards, though, I told her she had to tell Callum the truth. He already half suspected anyway, and it's been clear all along that he had never got over their break-up.'

'I'm not sure she's ready to tell him, even now. She looked mortified when he started asking about Kyle's birthday.'

He smiled. 'I think she was perturbed more because he said it in front of everyone. Callum's a bit like your father in that respect—he says things as he sees them and thinks about it afterwards.'

She laughed. 'I hope they manage to sort things out, anyway.'

'They'd better.' Ben was frowning now. 'I've had to keep my feelings on hold for what seems like ages, all because Anna refused to let me speak up. But not any more.' He looked her in the eyes. 'You have to know that I'm in love with you, Jassie.'

She stared at him, her eyes widening. 'Are you? Really?'

'Really. I think I've always been half in love with you from when you were a teenager, but there wasn't a thing I could do about it back then. Our lives were taking separate paths, and you were just starting out on your medical career. Then when you came back into my life, I just knew I had to make you mine.'

He ran his hand over her face, lightly caressing her cheek, drawing her towards him with infinite care until their lips met in a tender, blissfully satisfying kiss. 'You can't imagine how hard it has been for me,' he said gruffly. 'I've wanted you so much. It was like torture to have you distance yourself from me. And yet I felt sure that you wanted me just as much as I wanted you. Am I right, Jassie?'

'Yes, you're right,' she whispered, sliding down from the barstool and moving into his embrace. 'I love you, Ben. It feels as though I've loved you for ever.'

He groaned raggedly and kissed her again,

his hunger building, his body moving against hers as though he would possess her, body and soul. His hands stroked her, gliding over her curves and tugging her into the warmth of his thighs. 'I've waited for this moment for so long,' he said huskily. 'I love you, Jassie. I want to marry you. Will you marry me? Will you be my wife?'

'I will.' Her heart was running over with happiness. 'Oh, yes. Please.'

They stayed locked in each other's arms for what seemed like an eternity. The outside world ceased to exist, and all either of them wanted was to be melded together as one for the foreseeable future.

'We'll be married in the village church and invite everyone we know,' Ben said softly against her cheek.

'That means the entire village, then,' she said with a laugh. 'Still, I dare say we'll manage to fit them all in somehow.'

He gently nuzzled the silky skin of her throat.

'And we'll live here, at Mill House, and bring up our children in this beautiful countryside.'

'That sounds absolutely wonderful to me.' She gazed up at him. 'But what about the job in Cheshire? How does that fit into things?'

'It doesn't. I've been talking to the consultant at Wellbeck, and they're looking for another registrar. I've been told the job's mine, if I want it.'

She smiled happily. 'And you do want it, don't you?'

'Oh, yes, definitely, I do. Life is going to be just perfect, Jassie. I love you, and we'll be man and wife just as soon as the arrangements can be made.' He hugged her tight. 'Sooner rather than later...or I might just blow a fuse.'

She snuggled against him, resting her cheek against his chest. 'That would never do.' She was thoughtful for a moment, and then said, 'I expect there will be another wedding fairly soon, if things go well for Callum and Anna.'

'I'm sure they will. They love one another, and it looks as though nothing will stop Callum from winning her back. His only problem is that he's working away...though I dare say I could offer to lease him the barn and stable block at a low enough price so that he could set up business in the village. The set-up is ideal for horticulture and landscaping, and if he plays his cards right, people will come from all over to buy specialty produce. In time, he could buy the place, if he wanted.'

She cupped his face in her hands. 'Now I know why it is that I want to marry you,' she said. 'You're simply the best man in the whole world.'

He laughed and scooped her up in his arms once more. 'Goes without saying,' he murmured. Then he lowered his head towards her, claiming her lips once more, and Jasmine snuggled into his embrace. This was where she belonged. Everything was perfect.

MILLS & BOON PUBLISH EIGHT LARGE PRINT TITLES A MONTH. THESE ARE THE TITLES FOR APRIL 2011.

NAIVE BRIDE, DEFIANT WIFE
Lynne Graham

NICOLO: THE POWERFUL SICILIAN
Sandra Marton

STRANDED, SEDUCED...PREGNANT
Kim Lawrence

SHOCK: ONE-NIGHT HEIR
Melanie Milburne

MISTLETOE AND THE LOST STILETTO
Liz Fielding

ANGEL OF SMOKY HOLLOW
Barbara McMahon

CHRISTMAS AT CANDLEBARK FARM
Michelle Douglas

RESCUED BY HIS CHRISTMAS ANGEL
Cara Colter